Ski the Hellers

Ski the Hellers

Elisabeth Waters

Marion Zimmer Bradley Literary Works Trust
PO Box 193473
San Francisco CA 94119-3473
www.mzbworks.com

ISBN-13: 978-1-938185-70-0
ISBN-10: 1-938185-70-6

A Publication of
The Marion Zimmer Bradley Literary Works
Trust
PO Box 193473
San Francisco, CA 94119-3473

www.mzbworks.com

Contents

INTRODUCTION

I wrote my first Darkover story "The Keeper's Price" in 1977, back when MZB was still letting fans play in her universe. In my case, however, she promptly rewrote my story, and it's now in her story collection *Marion Zimmer Bradley's Darkover*. So is "Firetrap," which I wrote in 1990 for *Domains of Darkover*; she rewrote that one too. There are five stories about Hilary Castamir in *Marion Zimmer Bradley's Darkover*, and I wrote the first draft of four of them before MZB redid them to fit her concept of Hilary. Well, Hilary was her character in the first place, so I'm not complaining.

I had much better luck with my next story, which I called "The Alton Gift"—not to be confused with the 2007 novel by the same title; the story is only 800 words long. She loved that one. Both stories went into the Darkover anthology *The Keeper's Price*. By then I was living in Berkeley and working for MZB, and as she continued to edit Darkover anthologies for DAW Books, I kept writing stories for them. I ended up with thirteen stories spread out over twelve anthologies, so I decided it was time to pull them together into one place. I wrote one more "short and funny" piece (MZB always liked to have one for the end of an anthology) and assembled this collection.

THE ALTON GIFT

I originally wrote this for a short story contest for MZB's fanzine *Starstone*. We needed to submit our stories anonymously, and I was pretty sure she could identify mine by the postmark, because I didn't think too many people in Connecticut were entering the contest. Fortunately I worked for a manufacturing company that had office all along the East Coast, along with two factories: the original one in Willimantic, CT and the newer one in Sevier, NC. So I put my story in the envelope, put stamps on it, and put it into the interoffice mail to one of my friends in Sevier to mail for me. Coincidently, her post office was in Marion, NC, so that was the postmark.

The contest had three judges, marking stories on a score of 1-30. Two judges gave me 30s, but the third hated the ending, so I came in second overall. After the judging, but before they had matched the stories with the authors, Marion came to visit us (she and my father were cousins). She was telling me about a story in the contest that showed not only talent but also technique, called "The Alton Gift." I carefully kept my face blank. Later during the visit she told me that since the stories had been judged, it was all right for me to tell her which one I wrote. When I said "The Alton Gift" she gasped and fell into the chair behind her. I'm glad the chair was there, but it might have been better if it had not been a rocking chair…

Caillean Alton finished lacing her dress and started to braid her hair, rather awkwardly, because this was only the third time she had tried to do it herself. Her hair had been cut short and offered to Evanda the day of the festival which marked Caillean's becoming a woman, and now that it just touched her collarbone and was long enough to braid again, she was considered fully grown and old enough to marry—which, Caillean thought bitterly, was the polite way of saying that now the *leroni* would decide where they wanted to fit her in their breeding program, and she would be given to the man as if she were a cow or a sheep—and they would call it "her duty to kinsmen and clan." Merciful Avarra!

Her mother entered her room just then, unannounced. Bianca Alton had borne nine children, five of whom had survived infancy and only two adolescence, and she overshadowed her children to the point where disobeying her never occurred to them. Caillean really wished that her mother would knock, or at least make a little noise in the hall, instead of appearing suddenly and making people jump, but she knew that nothing was ever going to make her mother change.

"Caillean, how long do you plan to take to braid your hair? You're already late for breakfast, and your father wants to talk to you right afterwards!"

Caillean hastily picked up her clasp and tried to fasten the end of the braid, but her hands slipped, and the whole mess began to unravel.

Muttering something Caillean did not quite catch about Durraman's donkey, Bianca quickly and efficiently braided her hair and slipped the clasp into place. "There! Come along, child, don't keep your father waiting."

After a hasty breakfast, Caillean found herself sitting opposite her parents in her father's study.

"Well, Caillean," her father smiled at her, "I'm sure you will be pleased to hear that a husband has been chosen for you. You will marry Dom Bertin Serrais next month."

"You are a very lucky girl," Bianca said. "Fine

family, lovely estate; it's an excellent match."

"But, Mother, I don't like him. And I don't really want to get married."

"Nonsense! Every girl wants to get married. And it doesn't matter if you like him or not—what does that have to do with marrying him?"

"I don't want to live the rest of my life with someone I don't even like!"

"Why do you *think* you don't like him?" Her father was obviously trying, with limited success, for an attitude of patience with girlish folly.

"He kissed me last Midwinter night, and I didn't like it and I wanted him to stop and he wouldn't even listen to me!"

"You should be flattered that he finds you attractive, child," her mother said sharply. "That will be a big help when you are married."

"But I don't want to marry him—or anybody! Look at what happened to Rafaella! She got married, and less than a year later she was dead!"

"Your sister was always sickly; you know that. Most women survive childbirth perfectly well; I always did. Now, Caillean, calm yourself; it is perfectly all right for a bride to be a bit nervous, but you must not make such a fuss that you displease Dom Bertin when he arrives."

"Mother, I am *not* going to marry him!"

"Don't be so childish, of course you are! Really, Caillean, you should be very thankful for your good fortune. It's not as though your *laran* were anything really useful, it's just something the *leroni* want to experiment with—and you're getting a very good husband out of all this, so I expect you to hold your tongue and behave like a properly brought-up young lady."

"Why can't you ever listen to me! You don't care how I feel—all you care about is yourself! I can be bred to Dom Bertin as if I were a sheep or something, and if I die the way Rafaella did, well, that's just too bad; you don't even care!" Caillean was screaming now. "I hate you! I wish *you* had died in childbirth!"

Bianca gave a slight gasp and suddenly slumped over, falling off her chair onto the floor. Caillean sat there, staring in astonishment, as her father bent over her mother's body. Then he turned his head and looked in fury at her.

"She's dead! You spawn of the cat-men, what did you do to her?"

Suddenly Caillean understood. So this was the *laran* that wasn't "really useful" but that the *leroni* wanted—the ability to kill with an angry thought. *That's absolutely all they need, another weapon for their continual wars. No, I won't let that happen.*

"What did you *do* to her?"

"Nothing very difficult, Father," Caillean said quietly. "Only this." And she reached inside her own body and stopped her heart.

REBIRTH

One of the things that was not a benefit of working on the Darkover anthologies was reading stories Marion loved and I didn't. There was a story in the line-up for *Sword of Chaos* that was a very good story but had a character so evil that it gave me nightmares. So I wrote this story as an antidote to it. Writing can be a very useful way to deal with your feelings.

Ann'dra whined as he woke from his nightmare and looked around the kennel, dimly lit by two of the four moons. All the other dogs were asleep around him, but they had the advantage of having been born dogs, while he, until a month ago, had been human, secretary to a neighboring lord. He had been captured by Dom Felix, lord of this castle, and tortured to make him reveal the information he had been copying. Rather than break under torture, he had left his body, and, knowing that Dom Felix would find him in the Overworld, he had hidden himself in the body of his hound. Unfortunately, Dom Felix had guessed what had happened, and Ann'dra still woke from nightmares seeing Dom Felix's malicious smile as he ordered the dog taken to the kennels and cut the man's throat.

Ann'dra scratched at a flea and tried to find a comfortable position. Being a dog certainly had its disadvantages, but at least he could no longer be forced to reveal the locations Dom Felix had wanted to send clingfire against. Filthy stuff. There must be better uses for *laran* than making clingfire and sending it out to burn crops, animals, and people indiscriminately, or spying, or all of the other things that the *leroni* did in the service of their warring lords. Well, at least *laran* could get him out of this flea-bitten body for a bit.

He slipped gratefully out of the dog's body and watched it curl up and settle back to sleep, animated now only by the dog's mind, then wandered into the castle. Checking on Dom Felix, he found him in bed, as he had expected, but neither Dom Felix nor his lady was asleep. Ann'dra, being no voyeur, was about to leave, when he noticed something that stopped him in his tracks. The lady was *raiva*, and new body was being created. Choosing his moment carefully, he merged with the embryo, taking the new body for his own and settling down to await rebirth.

"What do you think it will be this time, Felix?"

the lady murmured sleepily.

"A son," Felix replied without hesitation. "He will be a *laranzu* and warrior, and no one will be able to stand against him, and he will be known as Varzil the Great!"

No, thought Ann'dra/Varzil. *No more wars. It's time to end the fighting.*

CHILD OF THE HEART

MZB made a rule that a Renunciate living in a Guildhouse could not keep any son she bore with her once he reached the age of five. While I can see that having teenage boys in a Guildhouse would be problematic, I still thought this would be rough on a five-year-old. So when I was told to write a story about a Free Amazon, I produced this.

Jamilla n'ha Gabriella lay in her bed feeling barely alive. She didn't have the energy to get up, in fact, she felt that she might never move again. Her mind told her that it was after sunrise and she should have gotten up when she woke up an hour ago, but the body simply refused to obey.

Keitha had explained to her that this was a perfectly normal feeling—they called it depression, and Jamilla could certainly see why. It was a consequence of the changes in her body from giving birth, and in Jamilla's case it was made worse by the fact that her baby had been a boy and she had given him to his father and his wife to raise. But Edrik had been born a month ago, surely she should be feeling better by now!

~oOo~

Booted footsteps came down the hall, and her oath-sister Perdita came rapidly into the room. "Jamilla, for Evanda's sake, get up! You know you'll feel better once you're up and moving—I can't understand why you lie in bed and brood for an hour every morning! And if you pull this on the trail tomorrow, I'll dump you out of your bedroll into the coldest stream I can find!"

Jamilla dragged herself out of bed and reached for her clothes, feeling the tears start to her eyes. Thinking rationally, she knew that Perdita loved her, they had done guide work together ever since the end of Jamilla's house-bound time. But at the moment she felt that she was a horrible person and that everyone hated her and that everyone was right to hate her.

As she was lacing up her tunic Perdita came over and patted her consolingly on the shoulder. "I'm sorry, Jamilla. I know you miss Edrik, but lying around thinking about it doesn't help. Why don't you go see him this morning—we don't have to leave until afternoon."

Jamilla tied the laces and reached for her belt. "I'm not going to see him, Perdita. It's better for him not to know me—that way he won't miss me."

"I'm not sure it works that way," Perdita shrugged, "but it's your business." She turned to the door. "I'll go start getting the supplies together. Be sure you eat a proper breakfast before you join me."

~o0o~

They got the supplies packed, ate dinner at the Guildhouse, and then went to pick up their charge—a nine-year-old boy going to study at Nevarsin. His father was a goldsmith and a friend of Perdita's, who took leave of his son with a long series of exhortations on proper conduct, ending with "...and don't give them any trouble, Coryn."

"Why should I, Father?" Coryn said with an air of wide-eyed innocence that positively screamed 'trouble!' "Aren't they my aunts?"

Jamilla raised an inquiring eyebrow at Perdita, who gave her an "I'll explain later" look, and they headed out of the city.

The road was wide enough near Thendara for them to ride abreast, and Jamilla tried to engage Coryn in conversation. "Are you excited about going to Nevarsin?"

"No."

"You've traveled before?"

"No."

He seemed very constrained by something.

"Are you nervous about the trip? It's really not all that bad."

"If it's not all that bad, why did my mother die on it?" Coryn snapped.

"Your mother?" Jamilla was startled.

"Mara n'ha Kindra," Perdita explained. "She died in a rock fall about five years ago. I knew her slightly; she was usually at Armida."

"If you knew her even slightly, that's more than I ever did," Coryn said bitterly. "She obviously didn't care to know me." Apparently this rankled, for he went on, "Father may think Renunciates are noble and wonderful, but I think she was a bitch. No doubt it would have been different if I'd been a girl, but since I was a boy I got thrown out like a whore's mistake! Your precious oath says that you're all mothers, sisters, and daughters to each other, but Zandru help any son of yours, for no one else will!"

He kicked his chervine and rode a bit ahead of them, while Perdita kept a wary eye on him. Jamilla continued to lead the pack animals, but she felt stunned and shocked. The cynicism and bitterness would have been dismaying in anyone; in a child of nine, they were appalling.

Coryn stayed ahead of them until they reached the first fork, when he fell back to ride behind Perdita while Jamilla and the pack animals brought up the rear, but he didn't utter a word for the rest of the day.

Unfortunately, that silence didn't extend to his sleep. Jamilla was having trouble sleeping, and when she finally did managed to doze off, she dreamed that her baby was crying for her. She tried to go to him, but she couldn't move, and the crying went on and on and on until she thought she would scream. And she was awake and the crying was still there. She crawled, shivering, over to Coryn's bedroll, and discovered that he was the source of the noise. He was sound asleep, and he was whimpering—the forlorn sound of an abandoned, hopeless child. Jamilla shook him gently, and he started up, banging his head into her jaw.

"Nightmare?" she asked sympathetically. "He looked sullenly at his lap and pressed his lips tightly together.

"Want to talk about it?"

"Why should I want to talk to you? You don't care about anything, you're just an Amazon. Do what you please, take off when things get inconvenient—I'm not going to trust you for anything!" He lay down with his back to her, and Jamilla returned to her bedroll and tried to stop shivering.

Was her son crying for her, she wondered, and would he feel, when he grew older, that she had abandoned him because she didn't want him?

Would he understand that she was doing what she really believed to be best for him, regardless of what it cost her? And was what she was doing the best thing to do?

She didn't hear Coryn cry again that night, but she wondered if he lay awake for the rest of it.

~o0o~

He was silent the next day, but started crying again in his sleep that night. Jamilla quietly moved her bedroll close to his, and very softly, being careful not to wake him, sang a lullaby. Apparently enough of it got through, for he stopped crying and slept peacefully. He gave her a strange look when he woke in the morning and found her near him, but he didn't say anything. And that night, when they made camp, he put his bedroll near hers—not as close as they had been in the morning, but much closer than the other side of the fire where he had started.

Over the next couple of days he became slowly more approachable; he began to ask questions about the route they were taking and the strange plants along the trail and why did the stars look so much brighter than they did in the city. It was the day before they were due to reach Nevarsin when they passed a gully littered with the remains of many rock-falls. At the moment the road was clear, but there was still enough of the mountain hanging overhead to make it plain that this could change at any time. Coryn looked very nervous as they rode through that section, and he carefully waited until they were out of it before asking, with studied casualness, "Is that where my mother died?"

"I believe so," Perdita replied, "but it's usually quite safe; I've been through there dozens of times. Anyway, we're through it now."

"Right." Coryn said. "All through it." But Jamilla noticed that he shivered for quite a while afterwards.

~o0o~

That night he put his bedroll so close to hers it was almost touching, and she wasn't surprised when the crying started. This time it escalated rapidly into sobs, followed by a scream of "Mother!"

Perdita, several feet away, woke up at that, but Jamilla, already gathering Coryn into her arms, shook her head, and Perdita lay down again.

"Mother, mother, don't leave me!" Coryn cried, still mostly asleep, but clinging desperately to her.

"It's all right, *chiyu*," Jamilla murmured soothingly. "I'm here, "I've got you, it's all right." She repeated the reassurances until the tight clutch relaxed and Coryn drifted back to sleep, then she tucked him, bedroll and all, carefully in beside her.

~oOo~

When she woke the next morning he was sitting beside her, watching her. "I had a funny dream last night," he announced. "I dreamed I was looking for my mother under all those rocks, and then there was this old woman—really old, older than anyone I've ever seen, and she said that all Renunciates were my mother because they were all sisters and daughters of the same mother—so does this mean that you're my mother?"

Jamilla smiled as she hugged him, "Yes, Coryn, that's what it means. That's what the Oath is about—it's not intended to cut us off from our families, it's supposed to make us all part of a bigger family."

And Edrik is still part of my family, she realized, *even if he is a boy and can't live with me—Edrik is still my child.* When she returned to Thendara she would see him, even if it was more painful for them both than a clean break. They would both come to terms with that; painful or not.

~oOo~

Coryn hugged her goodbye at the entrance to Nevarsin Monastery, and hugged Perdita too "because if Jamilla's my mother, you're my aunt." Then Jamilla and Perdita started on the trip back to Thendara—and their other son and nephew.

PLAYFELLOW

This has the distinction of being the only story I wrote about Hilary Castamir that MZB did not take and rewrite. Because she didn't write any of it, she didn't put it in her story collection, so it's here in mine.

The trouble with working in a tower, Damon Ridenow thought ruefully, is that some things are impossible to keep secret, and our resident "ghost" definitely falls into that category.

Fortunately the circle had finished its night's work before ten-year-old Hilary Castamir, their newest technician, had voiced her desire for some dried fruit. Not that this was at all unreasonable; it was customary to eat something sweet after the grueling matrix work—but it was unusual for a bar of pressed dried fruit to suddenly materialize on the table under the eyes of six startled *leroni*. And Hilary clearly hadn't teleported it there; she was so tired she was barely able to murmur thanks, pick it up, and chew on it.

Damon, who had been working as monitor for the circle, quickly went to the cupboard to get fruit bars for the rest of the circle. He handed the first one to Leonie, Keeper of Arilinn Tower, as always being careful not to touch her. He was dismayed to see that her hand was trembling.

She shouldn't be this tired, he thought, using his *laran* to check her condition more closely; as monitor, he was responsible for the physical well-being of the people in the circle. Her heart was beating more rapidly than normal, her breathing was quicker than it should have been, and she was watching Hilary, who sat innocently munching on her fruit bar, with real dread. *She's afraid*, Damon realized in shock; *Leonie is afraid of the ghost—or whatever it is.*

But Leonie was a proud, strong, self-controlled woman. She dismissed the members of the circle to their beds in a calm voice, and only Damon guessed how much effort it cost her.

~oOo~

Damon went to bed deeply troubled. He loved Leonie, despite his attempts to convince himself that his feelings were merely the respect due the Lady of Arilinn. To him, Leonie was Arilinn; he could not imagine a Tower without her. He wanted to nothing more thing to see her well and happy. *And if that means getting rid of this ghost*, he thought, *so be it*.

Having come to this resolve, he slept, heedless

of the sun rising past his window.

~oOo~

Damon woke in the late afternoon, confused by fleeting fragments of a dream in which he had been running away from Nevarsin Monastery— wearing only a light tunic and barefoot in the snow, of all silly things. The dream had been terrifyingly real, but his conscious mind promptly dismissed it for the nonsense it was. He had never even been to Nevarsin; his family was not *cristoforo*. He had been taught at home until it was time for him to do his stint as a cadet and then an officer in the Comyn Guard. He had not been much of a soldier, but he had done his best with the role expected of a Comyn son. But nobody had been more relieved than he when he proved to have enough *laran* to enter service at Arilinn Tower at the age of seventeen. His years here had been happy ones; his fellow *leroni* were all the friends and family he needed, and he was a top matrix technician.

He dressed and went to the conservatory to enjoy what remained of the afternoon sun. As he approached, he heard a girl's voice softly singing an old ballad, and when he entered the room he saw Hilary sitting in the middle of the floor playing jackstones against herself. At least, he hoped so—there was no one else in the room, so the two uneven piles of stones must both belong to her.

"Hello, Hilary" he smiled at her. "Would you like another player?"

"Please," Hilary replied, looking up at him. "But I hope you're at least a little bit out of practice, Gregori's been beating me all afternoon."

"Gregori?" Damon sat on the floor beside her. Strange, both piles of stones had been pushed together in one heap, but he hadn't seen Hilary touch them.

"Don't you know Gregori?" Hilary asked, puzzled. "He's been around ever since I came to Arilinn."

"Who or what is Gregori?" Damon demanded.

"Well," Hilary struggled for words, "he's just Gregori." She thought a moment, then added, "he finds things when people lose them."

"And produces dried fruit bars on demand?"

"Request." Hilary corrected him primly. "It's not polite to demand things."

"True enough," Damon conceded. *This is a crazy conversation.* "Where did he come from?"

"I don't know," Hilary said. "He's been here longer than I have." She gathered up the jackstones, tossed them deftly from palm to back of hand, and started her turn.

They played in silence for Hilary's turn and then Damon's turn, but when he handed the ball back to her after his turn, she said, "No, it's Gregori's turn," and held up the ball. To Damon's amazement, *something* took the ball from her fingers, tossed the jackstones, and set the ball to bouncing.

Hilary is right, Damon thought dazedly as he watched, trying to believe what he was seeing. *Whatever it is, it's a terrific jackstones player.*

"If you want to know where Gregori came from," Hilary said, returning to their conversation, "why don't you ask him?"

Why not? Damon thought. Aloud he said, "Gregori, where did you come from?" Feeling like a fool, he listened, but heard nothing but the bouncing of the ball. He looked questioningly at Hilary.

"Can't you hear him?" she asked. Damon shook his head. "Oh," she frowned, "that's odd. I wonder why not. Anyway, he said 'Nevarsin'."

Fortunately for what remained of Damon's peace of mind, they were interrupted before he had a chance to consider the implications of Gregori's origin combined with his dream. Flora, the circle's third technician, came in and said, "Damon, Leonie wants to see us."

Leonie, as it turned out, wished to discuss Hilary. "She's made great progress in the short time she's been with us, and I believe we can make a Keeper of her."

Damon bit back an instinctive protest. Being a Keeper, as they all knew, was a hard life, and Hilary was just a child. Of course, Leonie had presumably been a child once, difficult as this now was to imagine.

Flora did protest. "It's really too soon to tell, and you can't begin training her seriously until her woman's cycles have started and become established."

"It is true that this is firmly decreed by custom," Leonie replied, "but we are in desperate need of Keepers in these days, and you well know, Flora, how many girls fail in the training." Damon knew, too; he had seen five of them in the time he'd then at Arilinn. "While I certainly am limited in the amount of training I can do while she is still a child, I believe that it is worthwhile to begin the training now. If nothing else, it will give her time to accustom herself mentally to being a Keeper; that may be enough to ensure that she succeeds."

"It may." Flora sounded thoughtful. "And she may mature sooner than we expect; she seems lately to be manifesting poltergeist activity— remember the fruit bar this morning?"

Leonie frowned. "I don't feel poltergeist activity is a sign of a future Keeper—and I don't think she produced the fruit bar, aside from asking for it."

"But what else could it be?' Flora asked.

"I don't know," Leonie replied, "and it worries me. I don't want anything in this Tower that I don't understand; it's too dangerous with the work we do."

"For what it's worth," Damon volunteered, "she says that it is somebody named Gregori, he's been here longer than she has, and he came from Nevarsin."

Both women looked at him incredulously. "Nevarsin?" Floria said. "Nevarsin doesn't train telepaths. Furthermore, if this Gregori is a person, where is he? He's obviously not on the physical plane, and I don't remember seeing anyone strange in the Overworld."

Leonie was more practical. "Well, if she can communicate with him, well and good. Damon, I want you to work with her, find out what this 'Gregori' is, and get rid of it. We need her too badly as a Keeper to have her playing around with—" she paused, uncertain "—whatever this is. I'll excuse both you and Hilary from the Circle, after tonight's working, so you can devote your time and energy to this, but please deal with it as quickly as possible. You're both needed in the Circle."

~o0o~

Damon didn't worry about Gregori again until early the next morning; the work of the matrix

31

circle didn't leave room to think about anything else. Hilary was monitor that night, so Gregori had no reason to teleport anything across the room to her, and Damon was quite sure that he was the only one seated so as to see that the tray of dried fruit met her halfway when she went to get it.

"Hilary?" he opened his mouth to tell her about their assignment, paused to chew a mouthful of his portion of dried fruit, and abruptly decided that dealing with Hilary and Gregori could wait until he'd had some sleep. "Leonie has excused us from tomorrow's circle; there's some research she wants us to do instead. Will you please wake me at mid-afternoon, if I'm not up by then?"

"Yes, Damon," Hilary nodded sleepily. "I'll see you then."

Damon dragged himself off to bed, collapsed into it, and promptly fell into a nightmare.

He was a young boy, wearing a rough homespun tunic, sitting on a bed in some sort of dormitory. All around him were boys, some younger than he was and some a year or so older and starting to grow hair on their faces. Three of the largest were confronting him.

"You think you're so smart, bastard—well, you're not; you're nothing! Son of a woman too stupid to know who fathered her child—"

"If she looked anything like him, she was too

ugly for anybody who lay with her to be willing to tell her his name! Look at that hair on him—he looks like he crawled out of Zandru's tenth hell!"

"Or maybe from under a rock," the third is snickered.

Damon sat there and kept quiet; part of him knew that if he ignored them they'd get tired after a while and leave him alone. But suddenly the biggest boy looked at him differently; the game was changing its rules.

"Of course, if he were a girl, he might be passable, in a delicate sort of way."

His followers obviously didn't understand, but they tried to play along anyway. "I don't know," one of them said, "he looks more like an icicle than anything else."

"Icicles can melt," the first boy replied, "if they get hot enough." He reached out toward Damon.

Damon felt something, some energy, pass through him. He wasn't sure what it was; it wasn't *laran*, exactly, and it wasn't a threshold sickness, though it felt somewhat like it. He felt his body rise to its feet and heard his voice say, "If you want heat—"

The tunic of the boy facing him went up in flames. Damon was conscious of a strong sense of satisfaction, of rightness. It was right that the bully should be running around the room screaming as the flames seared his flesh; this was what he had wanted, wasn't it? He'd been hot, and searching for an answering fire in Damon, hadn't he?

The other boys were screaming, too, and the novice master came running in and rolled the boy in a blanket to smother the flames. As they went out, the force holding Damon in place released him, and he sat down abruptly on the bed.

The prior arrived, alerted by all the noise. A dozen boys hastened to tell him that "it was all Gregori's fault, Bevin was just talking to him, honest, and he set him on fire, he's a devil—"

The prior shook them off without a word, and stalked over to the cot where Damon was still sitting, thoroughly confused. Was he Gregori, then?

The prior grabbed him by one shoulder, his bony grip painful on unhealed bruises that Damon hadn't noticed before. Still saying nothing, although his face was an eloquent indicator of his distaste, he dragged Damon/Gregori to the front gate of the monastery and flung him forth. "Go join your father in hell, boy; it's plain you don't belong among those who follow the Holy Bearer of Burdens." He slammed the gate shut.

Damon rose to his feet and stumbled down the road warmed by the late afternoon sun. *At least*, he thought, I *don't need to worry about direction; from Nevarsin all roads lead south.*

And another voice inside him said, I *don't want*

to go to hell; I'm going to Arilinn. So Damon—or Gregori—headed toward Arilinn.

He walked, putting one foot in front of the other. He was soon out of Nevarsin and walking alone down the road. It was getting dark when he heard a troupe of riders coming along behind him. He hid behind a tree, so they wouldn't see him. He didn't want anyone to see him; they'd only be angry at him, everyone got angry at him…

It was getting dark quickly now, but Damon thought that the riders were women, all wearing crimson tunics like some sort of uniform. They passed too quickly for him to be sure though, and he went back to the road once they were out of sight and continued to walk south. It was cold, but three of the moons were out, so there was light enough to walk.

He walked quickly so that the cold wouldn't get him; he walked until he was too tired for the cold to bother him; he walked until he was falling over with weariness. He crawled off into a hollow at the side of the road and slept. As he fell asleep some small bit of his mind told him he shouldn't sleep in the snow, but he was too tired to care.

When he woke things were gray and foggy; he couldn't see much of anything other than the road. But he could make out the road quite clearly, and he felt much better. His body didn't ache and wasn't cold and didn't seem to slow him down at all. He went on down the road, and on, and on, and on…

The road seemed to last forever, and he'd lost track of how long he'd been following it, but finally he saw it—Arilinn Tower, gleaming in the sun, the most beautiful sight in all the world.

And Hilary was calling him. "Damon? Damon, wake up! Damon, you told me to wake you up at mid-afternoon."

He pried grainy eyelids open and looked up at her. The view from his window was shadowed, which meant the sun had moved to the other side of the tower. *It must be quite late in the afternoon*, he thought, struggling to orient himself.

"Hilary?" She was looking at him, obviously concerned. "Go down to the kitchen and get me some *jaco*, will you?" She nodded quickly and left. Damon dragged himself out of bed and managed to get some clothes on before she returned, bearing a tray with a pitcher of steaming liquid and a mug. Damon took it gratefully, collapsed in one chair with it, and waved her to another.

She curled up, kitten-like, wrapping her skirts around her feet. "What's happening, Damon? What does Leonie want us to do?"

"She's worried about Gregori, Hilary. Being new to the Tower, you may not realize it, but it is not the custom for a Tower to have a resident poltergeist."

Hilary sat for a moment with her head a bit to one side, obviously listening. "He says he's not going back to Nevarsin. They don't like him there." She frowned and continued on her own, "Why doesn't Leonie like him?"

"Leonie doesn't dislike him; she's a merely concerned that he's interfering with your training. She wants to train you as a Keeper."

Hilary's eyes opened wide. "Me? A Keeper?" Her voice was reverent, as if they were offering to make her Queen in Thendara. Well, Keeper of Arilinn was just as high a rank.

"And she's concerned for him, too." Damon went on, suddenly remembering something. "Hilary, ask him who the women were on the road, the ones in the red tunics."

Hilary listened, looking blank. "What's the Sisterhood of the Sword?" she shook her head. "No, I don't know; I've never heard of them." She listened for several minutes, then turned to Damon. "They seem to be something like the Renunciates."

"Hilary," Damon said gently, "Gregori, the Sisterhood of the Sword hasn't been in existence for over two hundred years."

"But Gregori's not that old!" Hilary protested.

"Gregori's dead," Damon said softly. "He died the first night on the road from Nevarsin. Remember, Gregori? You lay down in the hollow beside the road and fell asleep, and when you woke up you were dead, but you were so determined to get Arilinn that you didn't notice. You didn't have the experience to realize that you'd left your body behind you and come on without it."

"Is that why nobody can see him?" Hilary asked in a small voice.

"Yes, that's why," Damon replied.

"What do we do now?" Hilary asked, and added, "Gregori wants to know."

"If you'll monitor for me, Hilary, I'll go out of body, meet him, and lead him to where he belongs now."

"Is it a bad place?" she asked anxiously.

"No," Damon reassured them. "Not at all."

"Can I come, too?" Hilary asked.

Damon shook his head. "I need you to monitor me; Leonie would be very cross with us both if I went out without a monitor. And where Gregori is going is too dangerous a place for the living; you don't have enough training yet to return safely."

"When I'm a Keeper, I'll be able to," she said. It was a statement, not a question.

"Yes, then. But not now."

"All right." Hilary rose and dragged to her chair over to the bed, while Damon lay down and arranged his body so that it would function during his absence. As he slipped free, he could hear Hilary thinking, *but I'm going to miss Gregori.*

He saw Gregori almost immediately, a small fragile boy with pale white hair dressed in a finer version of the rough tunic he had worn it Nevarsin.

"You say I've been dead for more than two centuries," he said. "Why do I have to leave now? I don't want to leave Hilary; she'll miss me."

"Yes, she will miss you," Damon agreed readily. "And I'll miss you, and even Leonie will miss you. You should be missed; nobody ought to die unnoticed and unmourned. But your work here is done, and your place is elsewhere now." He pointed to a glow in the distance. "We go that way." He started slowly toward the light, and, after a brief pause, Gregori followed him.

They walked, or perhaps floated, for a time, then Gregori spoke. "Will you take care of Hilary for me?"

"Hilary's growing up, Gregori; she can take care of herself. But I shall certainly be her friend."

"Is she still allowed to have friends if she's a Keeper?"

"If she allows herself to, yes," Damon said, thinking of Leonie, who didn't seem to think she was allowed to have anyone.

"I hope she will," Gregori said. "She's nice. I liked her." He didn't seem to notice he'd used the past tense. "It's getting warmer," he added in surprise. "I've been cold for so long." He looked around him. "It's so beautiful—can you hear the singing?"

Damon could, very faintly, and he knew it was time for him to turn back. Already he was beginning to feel he could stay here forever, soaking in the warmth and the light, listening to the singing until he learned enough to join in … he shook himself. "Can you find your way from here, Gregori?"

"Oh, yes," Gregori said absently. "Give my love to Hilary. Fare well, Damon."

"Fare thee well, Gregori."

"I shall." Gregori passed him, heading farther into the light. Damon caught himself starting to follow him, wanting to follow him. He shook his head violently.

He was back in his own body, with his head aching as if it were being split apart, feeling as if he'd fallen all the way back.

Hilary was bending over him. "You look awful!" she whispered. Damon was very glad she was having that much consideration for his headache.

"It's hard to get back from there." He whispered, too. "Gregori sends you his love. He's found where he belongs, and he's happy."

"I'm glad," Hilary said. "But I will miss him."

Her gray eyes filled with tears. "Now I won't have anyone to play with."

"You should miss him," Damon agreed. "Nobody should die unmissed—no wonder he didn't realize he was dead."

"Do you suppose Leonie will miss him?"

"I'm sure of it," Damon said. *No need to say that she'll be happy to miss him.*

Hilary brightened. "If I'm a Keeper, I won't have time to play with Gregori anyway. But I'm still going to miss him."

"So am I," Damon said, surprised to realize that he truly would.

SIN CATENAS

I often get story ideas from casual mentions of something in one of the Darkover novels. This one came from the very brief reference to *Domna* Crystal Castamir in *Forbidden Tower*. Like several of my other stories, it started with my wondering how her child would react to the situation.

Veradis Castamir chose her husband when she was nine years old. It was, of course, a serious decision. She was the only daughter of Lady Crystal Castamir and her husband, Dom Ruyven of Castamir, and thus heiress to all Lady Crystal's estates—or at least such portion of them as survived Dom Ruyven's profligacy. Some men, Veradis knew, hunted forests into deserts, some gambled every coin and jewel they could lay their hands on, some drank until they were nothing but shaky shells. Dom Ruyven had a different hobby. He fathered bastards.

For as long as Veradis could remember, her father had had some girl or other living with them, each younger and dumber than the last. One would last about a year, then the current one would be married off to some small farmer or craftsman, with a dowry to support the bastard the girl was carrying, and Dom Ruyven would get a new girl and start over. Lady Crystal might not like it, but there wasn't much she could do—he was her husband—and she was too much a lady to do other than put a good face on the whole mess. Veradis wasn't so forbearing, which was why she was currently hiding in the woods.

Even in a life full of unfortunate incidents, today's had been particularly so. Veradis had disliked Asharra, her father's latest *barragana*, from the day she arrived, three years ago. What he saw in the woman Veradis couldn't imagine, but for some reason he had kept her, even when she bore him a daughter. Lady Crystal was fostering the brat, saying bravely how nice it was to have a baby in the house. Veradis thought it must be bad enough to get up at night to quiet your own screaming baby, but having to do it for someone else's, while she lay in bed with your husband, was intolerable. And today Asharra had come up to Veradis and announced, with a truly idiotic smirk, that Veradis was going to have another sister. Veradis had looked her straight in the eye, making no effort to hide her disgust, and said, "You are mistaken; I am an only child."

Unfortunately, her father had entered the

room just then, overheard her, and beat her severely for 'discourtesy to her elders.' And her mother had cried over her and said that it was a woman's lot to accept whatever her husband chose to do.

Veradis, being in pain and thoroughly out of temper, had snarled back, "That makes it all the more important to choose a husband for something other than his good looks!" Her mother dissolved into floods of tears, and Veradis escaped to the woods to do her own crying in decent privacy.

~o0o~

Now she lay carefully on one side by the edge of a stream—she knew she wasn't going to want to sit down for several days at least—rinsing her face, and sobbing. "I just can't live like this!"

"In the woods?" a voice behind her said lightly. "I shouldn't think so; it gets too cold at night."

Startled, Veradis incautiously rolled over, yelped with pain, and struggled hastily to her knees. She faced a boy about her own age, dressed in clothes that, while plain, appeared to have been clean and neat before he spent most of the day in the woods.

"Are you injured?" he asked with obvious concern.

"Not really," Veradis sighed. "Just a beating, not the first, and I'm very much afraid not the last either."

"But why would anyone beat you?" he asked incredulously.

"My father didn't like the way I spoke to his *barragana*."

"Oh. You're Lady Crystal's daughter then."

"My father's activities must be notorious indeed," Veradis sighed. "I've never even seen you before, and you can identify me just from knowing that my father beat me because I was rude to his *barragana*."

"Well, I don't know your name," he admitted, "but my aunt did mention your mother as an example of—well, uh, ladylike endurance?"

"Idiotic stupidity?"

"I was trying to avoid saying that. My name's Cullen, and I've come to live with my aunt, who is married to the tanner."

"My name is Veradis, and I'm happy to meet you. What happened to your parents?"

Cullen bit his lip. "My father is dead, and my mother's a Renunciate, so I can't live with her."

"Whyever not? What's a Renunciate?"

"Renunciates are women who swear never to marry or be supported by men, so they live together in what they call Guildhouses, and boys aren't allowed to live there after they turn five."

"That's awful! Well, I can understand wanting to get away from men, but giving up your child..."

"Yeah." Cullen stared at the ground. "I wish my mother agreed with you. Children shouldn't have to live like this."

"No," Veradis agreed. "They shouldn't. Children are supposed to be a valuable gift from the Goddess, but the way some parents act, you'd think we were worth less than a rabbithorn!" To her surprise, she suddenly started crying again. "I hate them!" she sobbed. "I hate my parents and I don't want to be like them, ever, but I'm afraid I'm going to be because I don't know how else to be, and I don't want to hate them—they're all the parents I've got—but my father's an arrogant lecher and my mother's a nothing who lets him kick her—and me!—around. I mean, if she wants to look after his bastards, that's her choice, but what about me? If she cared about me at all, she'd at least send me away to be fostered somewhere, but when the *leronis* who tested me last spring suggested it, Mother said she couldn't possibly give me up! And I don't even have enough *laran* to go to a Tower—if Mother had to marry a man who'd abuse her, couldn't she at least have gotten one with *laran*?"

Cullen knelt beside her, held her against his chest, and patted her very gingerly on the shoulder. "Your father is a fool. He should be proud to have a daughter as beautiful as you are."

"And your mother should be proud to have a son as nice as you are," Veradis said, picking her head up and mopping her eyes with the edge of her shawl.

Cullen chuckled. "Well, at least we agree on the important things. Shall we get married when we grow up?"

Veradis looked at him in surprise, and watched as an older version overlay the boy's face in front of her. Suddenly she knew that this was what lay ahead for them, that they would marry and have children and grow old together. "Yes," she said solemnly, "when we grow up."

He looked at her and nodded slowly, and she wondered if he saw what she did. She shivered and realized it was getting dark. "I'd better go back before they miss me," she said.

"Right," he said. "We don't want a search party finding this place; we'll need it again."

She stood up and wrapped her shawl tightly around her. Just one question, Cullen," she said, smiling impishly. "You don't have any desire to be a father to your country, do you?"

Cullen laughed. "No, Veradis," he said, "the only children I want to father are yours. That will be plenty for me."

~oOo~

With her decision made, and with a place to escape to and someone to talk with, Veradis found life at home rather more bearable. It helped a lot to have a goal; she kept her mouth shut, and concentrated on learning all she could about housekeeping. She'd need to know it when she married Cullen. After her mother's death, of course, the Castamir estates would be hers, but there would probably be years when she and Cullen would have to live elsewhere, without any support from her parents. She had no illusions as to what her parents would think of her marriage, but they couldn't possibly think less of it than she thought of theirs!

She also learned how to take care of children; Dom Ruyven and Asharra provided her with plenty of practice. Over the next five years the number of their bastards grew from one to five. Lady Crystal seemed to age quickly and became less and less able to look after all the children. Fortunately, Veradis discovered that she liked babies and was good with small children, though she certainly would have preferred her own. Still, their unfortunate parentage wasn't the children's fault, and they were going to have enough trouble in their lives without having Veradis add to it.

She and Cullen continued to meet secretly in the woods, and if they saw each other in town when Veradis went there on errands they pretended not to know each other. Cullen had been apprenticed to the tanner, and had worked hard and learned the trade well. By the time they were fourteen, Cullen was capable of earning a living and Veradis could run a house.

"So, when shall we marry?" Veradis asked one autumn day as they sat talking in the woods.

"As soon as we're both fifteen," Cullen said. "I asked my mother when she last came up to visit me what the law was on Freemate marriages—I assume your parents aren't going to consent to our marrying *di catenas*?"

"I think that's a safe assumption," Veradis agreed. "That's why I've been careful not to let them know we even know each other. We don't want them looking for you when I disappear."

"Agreed," Cullen said. "I'll be visible earning a living, but you can be hidden pretty well—it's easier to find a tanner than it is to find someone who's not tied down to one trade."

"Do you think 'wife' isn't a trade?"

"Of course it is, but it's such a common one that it's harder to find one particular one." He made a face at her. "You know perfectly well what I mean. Don't be so difficult!"

"Sorry." Veradis grinned. "It's such a lovely change from meek and obedient daughter."

"Not too much longer now. I'll be fifteen next month, and you'll be fifteen in the spring."

Veradis nodded. "Our only problem is how soon my father will try to marry me off. Supporting his bastards is getting expensive, and as long as I'm heir to Castamir, I'm a rich prize for any of his friends willing to pay for the privilege."

Cullen nodded. "If he tries, you'll have to play for time. If we marry before you're fifteen, it won't be legal."

Veradis sighed. "If I'm lucky, he's forgotten how old I am. It's a good thing I'm small for my age. What's the form for Freemate marriage? Do we need witnesses?"

"Not really. The simplest form is for us to share a meal, a bed, and a fire. Freemate marriage isn't valid until it's consummated, so the sooner we have a child, the better."

"Yes, that does tend to indicate that a marriage has been consummated."

"And once we have a child, the Comyn Council can't dissolve the marriage."

"Oh." Veradis thought that one over. "I shouldn't think they would; the Castamirs are just a minor branch of the Hasturs—but I certainly don't want to take the chance. It's a good thing we both want children anyway. So we'll elope on my fifteenth birthday, and have our first child as soon as we possibly can. Any ideas as to where we should go?"

"I've been thinking about that," Cullen said

slowly. "You probably won't like this idea, but I think I should leave as soon as I turn fifteen, set up somewhere south of here, and come back for you in the spring. That way, we won't both disappear together. I've been talking to my aunt and uncle about my desire to go out and 'make my own way in the world' so they won't associate my going with you."

"You're right on both counts," Veradis said. "I'll miss you horribly, but it's a good plan and you should go. Then when I leave, nobody will even know you were here. Just don't lose track of the days."

"Don't worry," Cullen smiled. "I haven't forgotten your birthday since we've known each other, and I certainly have extra reason to remember it this year."

"True enough," Veradis smiled bravely. "I'll meet you here at dawn on my birthday." She hugged him hard.

~oOo~

On the eve of her fifteenth birthday, however, Dom Ruyven called Veradis into his study and informed her that he had chosen a husband for her. Mindful of the undesirability of open defiance, Veradis temporized.

"But, *vai dom*, I can't possibly leave. My lady mother needs me here to run the household."

This was at least partially true; Lady Crystal rarely left her bed at all now.

"Nonsense," he said briskly. "Asharra can run the place." Veradis stared at him in astonishment. *Whatever is he using for brains? Aside from the gross impropriety of setting his mistress up as lady of the house, there are serious practical problems.* Aloud she said simply, "But Asharra hasn't any aptitude at all for household management."

"How much does she need?" he snapped back. "Isn't that what a housekeeper is for?"

"It isn't that simple, *vai dom*," Veradis said quietly, trying to maintain the appearance of filial obedience.

"Well, you'll just have to teach her then," he said. "You can stay here for a while after the wedding if necessary. Your husband is a cousin of Asharra's; he won't mind—it's all family, after all."

That did it. Wise or not, there was only so much Veradis was capable of tolerating. She lifted her head, looked him straight in the eye, and said firmly, "Asharra is not a member of this family!"

"Oh, yes, she is," he retorted, "and she'll be even more so once you're married to her cousin."

"I won't marry him."

"Nonsense, of course you will. Every girl dreams of marriage—and surely you want children."

"Yes, I do." Her lips thinned tightly together.

"My children, not my husband's annual bastards!"

His lips tightened ominously, but she went on. "I've spent my whole life watching my mother house and feed your mistresses and care for your bastards—on her own estate! You chose well for your wife, but I'm not cut of the same cloth. I will not marry Asharra's cousin—or any other man you choose!"

He sprang from his chair with a snarl and slapped her hard across the face. "How dare you address me like that? That is not the way to address your father!"

"And your behavior is certainly no way to persuade me to marry anyone you approve of!" she pointed out, at the top of her lungs. "For my children, I want a father who doesn't think his job is done at the moment of conception!"

He grabbed her shoulder and shook her like a rag doll, shouting incoherently with rage. Veradis braced herself for a beating, hoping he wouldn't cause enough damage to stop her from traveling. *When, oh when*, she thought ruefully, *am I going to learn to control my temper and keep my mouth shut?*

Then she realized that the pounding noise she was hearing wasn't the blood in her head; someone was knocking at the study door. Dom Ruyven dropped her, fortunately into the chair she had been sitting in, flung open the door, and snarled at the steward. "You had better have a good reason for interrupting us!"

"I have," the man said curtly, looking disapprovingly at him. He crossed to Veradis and bowed to her. "I regret to inform you, *vai domna*, that your mother is dead."

Veradis didn't faint, not exactly, but everything went black momentarily and then came back in muted colors and she felt very cold. There were more people in the room now; the housekeeper was patting her hands and saying, "she didn't suffer, *chiya*; died quietly in her sleep she did."

"Yes," Veradis said faintly, "she was always quiet." The steward came over with a glass of brandy and held it to her lips. Veradis took a gulp of it, choked a bit, and came back to full awareness of her surroundings.

Her father, looking suitably grief-stricken, came and tried to slip an arm around her shoulder. She shrugged it off. "My dear child," he said. "Don't worry about your marriage for now. Plenty of time for that when we're over the worst of our grief."

Veradis stood up and looked at him in contempt. "You must think I'm quite lack-witted. I've had ample evidence over the years of your feelings for me, and I believe I've made my feelings toward you quite plain this evening. You—and Asharra, if she cares to stay with you now that you're no longer lord of the estate—can live in Windmill Cottage. The tenant died in the late fall, so it may need a bit of repair, but I'm sure it can be made livable by the time the funeral is over."

She glanced at the steward, who said, "With pleasure, *vai domna*."

"Good." She nodded at him, then turned back to her father. "The cottage is a bit small for all the children, so, if you like, I'll keep the ones already living here. If you father any more of them, however, they're your problem. Now, if you'll excuse me, I have work to do."

She was busy working for the rest of the night. First her mother's body had to be washed, dressed in her best festival gown, and laid out in the household chapel. Then, after snatching a few minutes to change into mourning, Veradis took over the study and started writing to all of the relatives who needed to be notified of the death and bidden to the funeral. The sky was beginning to grow light when she finally laid down her pen, stood up, and stretched. She snatched up her cloak, told the steward she was going out for a walk, and went to meet Cullen.

He was there before her, pacing nervously. She called his name and ran into his arms.

"Veradis, what's wrong?" he asked, holding her shaking body. "You don't have your things— what's happened?" He held her away to look at her face and saw her clothing. "Who?"

"My mother." To her surprise, Veradis started crying. "Last night."

"Merciful Avarra." Cullen sat down on a nearby log, cradling her in his arms.

"I don't know why I'm crying," Veradis sobbed. "She wasn't a very good mother; all she ever cared about was my father, and he didn't care for her, and it's all so sad..."

"Speaking of your father—"

"I told him that he and his *barragana* could live in Windmill Cottage."

Cullen chuckled. "Good for you. With all those children?"

"No, I'm keeping the children. They don't deserve this." She twisted her head to look at his face. "Do you mind if they live with us?

"No, of course not. Poor brats, what chance would they have with him? With his temper, shut up in a small cottage—he'd probably kill a couple of them." Both Cullen and Veradis shuddered, easily able to visualize that picture. "But—'with us'? Do you still want to marry me, now that you don't have to? I'm sure that your Hastur relatives would be happy to arrange a marriage for you, and surely not all Comyn men are like your father."

Veradis smiled and reached up to stroke his cheek. "Yes, Cullen, I still want to marry you. I've wanted to for six years, and I haven't changed my mind overnight. My mother made her choice, my father made his, and I've made mine, which is by far the best of the three."

A PROPER ESCORT

MZB carefully wrote guidelines for each year's anthology. One of her writers considered it a challenge to take something forbidden in the guidelines and turn it into a story that Marion couldn't bear to turn down. This is as close as I ever came to doing that, and it's not as if I didn't give Marion plenty of warning.

For several years she rejected (and complained about) two categories of stories that she referred to as "Subject A: a Free Amazon finds a man she can love and trust" and "Subject B: Dyan Ardais finds a woman he can love and trust." After a year or two of that, I started threatening to write Subject AB: Dyan Ardais and the Free Amazon. When the year's anthology title was *Renunciates of Darkover*, and I needed a Free Amazon story, I went ahead and wrote this.

Linnea n'ha Marilla sat quietly in the gatehouse at

Nevarsin under the disapproving eye of the porter. She wondered whether it was Renunciates the monk disliked or simply women in general. The sun had shifted noticeably to the west during the time she had been sitting there, and she hoped that the Abbot had by now at least received the message she had carried in such haste from Ardais. Lady Rohana of Ardais had sent Linnea to fetch her grandson, Dyan Ardais, home from his studies at Nevarsin so that she could bid him farewell before she died—an event which was expected to occur within the tenday. Linnea had been three days on the road from Ardais— although "road" was a rather generous description of the route she had taken, and she wanted to collect the boy quickly and start the journey back before dark and the threatening snowstorm arrived.

Sandaled footsteps scraped along the stone pathway, and a stooped white-haired monk entered. "You are *Domna* Rohana's messenger, *mestra*?" he asked politely. Linnea nodded, and he continued "I am Brother Harrel the guest-master. Please forgive me for not having come to welcome you sooner; I only just learned you were here. If you will come with me, I'll find you some supper and a bed for the night."

"That is most kind of you, Brother," Linnea replied, matching his polite tones. "But I am afraid that you may not have been informed of the urgency of my errand. Lady Rohana is failing rapidly, and Dyan and I must leave as soon as we possibly can. I had hoped," she added, "that he would be ready by now—surely he doesn't have that much to pack."

Brother Harrel looked distressed. "But, *mestra*, it will be dark in less than three hours! You can't drag a boy of his age out on the trail this late in the day—and you may not realize that it is going to snow tonight."

I do indeed realize that it is going to snow tonight, Brother," Linnea said grimly. "That is precisely why I wish to leave immediately. I grew up not a league south of here, and I know the signs of a storm that will undoubtedly block the pass for at least the next three days. We do not have that much time to spare; we must leave immediately." He looked dubious, so she added, "Lady Rohana's order does say to bring Dyan with all possible speed."

Brother Harrel looked even more unhappy. "I shall go to Father Abbot about this," he said, hurrying away to dump the problem of this stubborn woman in someone else's lap.

"I can't imagine what the boy's father is thinking of," the porter grumbled *sotto voce*, "not to be sending a proper escort for the boy."

Linnea ignored him, firmly suppressing her

first impulse to retort that the only thing on *Dom* Kyril's mind was the nearest bottle of wine. She hoped that Dyan did not resemble his father too much—if he did, he would prove a most unpleasant traveling companion.

Brother Harrel must have run all the way to the Abbot's office. In a surprisingly short time Linnea heard his voice in the hall, protesting to the Abbot that journeying in this weather was madness. The two men entered the gatehouse together, the Abbot holding Lady Rohana's order in his hand, and while he looked no happier about it than Brother Harrel, he did not seem as disposed to dismiss it out of hand.

"*Mestra*," he gave her brief courteous nod, "is this really necessary? Can't you wait until the storm passes?"

Linnea shook her head. She had seen Lady Rohana herself when she received the order, and she prayed the woman was still alive even now. Her order was clear, and she was going to obey it. "The Lady of Ardais has sent for Lord Dyan, and she wishes him to travel with all possible speed. Spending three or four days here waiting out the snowstorm that's coming does not fit my definition of "all possible speed"—and the longer you delay our departure, the greater our chances of getting trapped in the pass. I'm not asking for your blessing, Father; I have a job to do, and I intend to do it—with your blessing, or without it!"

"And if the Lady of Ardais has sent for me, it is my duty to obey her summons."

Linnea started; she had not seen the boy come through the archway. By his speech, this must be Lord Dyan Ardais, but he bore no resemblance to the rest of his family—or indeed, to most of the Comyn. Instead of the red hair common to his caste, his was dark, his eyes were a steely gray, and he was slight in stature. Linnea knew him to be ten years old, but he appeared younger, except for the calm, graceful air of the born nobleman.

"Dyan, my boy," the Abbot began, "we all appreciate your desire to attend your grandmother in her illness, but you do not have to rush out into an oncoming storm," he gestured to the window, which now showed only overcast sky with barely a hint of the sun's position, "with only a single woman to escort you. We can provide a suitable escort of lay brothers and guards for you as soon as the storm passes."

Dyan regarded him with a carefully expressionless face. "Lady Rohana has been ill for months, Father Abbot," he said politely. "If she sends for me now in haste, she is dying; and I shall leave at once with her chosen escort." Another boy, this one with the red hair of Comyn, appeared behind Dyan, carrying two saddlebags.

"Kennard," said the Abbot, "you should be at

your studies at this hour."

"Yes, Father," the boy agreed meekly, handing the bags to Dyan and embracing him. "Safe journey, *bredu*." Dyan returned the embrace without speaking, and Kennard left them.

The Abbot sighed. "If, as you say, *mestra*, the storm is almost upon you, I suppose you had best leave at once. And if you are determined to go—with or without my blessing—you shall go with it." He rested his hand first on Dyan's head and then on Linnea's. "May the Holy Bearer of Burdens bless and strengthen you in your journey."

"Thank you, Father," Linnea said formally. Then she turned to the boy. "If you're ready, Lord Dyan, the chervines are in the courtyard." Dyan nodded briefly, shouldered his bags, and preceded her out the door.

They mounted and road at their best pace through the pass, but even so, the snow was thick on the ground and beginning to block the way by the time they won through.

"Do you have *laran*, *mestra*?" Dyan asked abruptly as they started down the other side of the pass. It was the first remark he had addressed to her, and Linnea suddenly realized that he probably didn't even know her name—in the haste of their departure, she had neglected a proper introduction.

"My name is Linnea, Lord Dyan," she said, "and you may call me that if you wish. And no, I don't have *laran*. Why would you think I might?"

Dyan looked faintly embarrassed; apparently he disliked being in error. "You told Father Abbot that the pass would be blocked, and he accepted your word for it—and you were correct."

"That's true," Linnea said conscious of a seemingly irrational desire to spare the boy's feelings and help him maintain his dignity—as if this self-possessed Comyn lordling needed much help in that direction. "I can see how such foreknowledge would look like *laran*, but in truth it's the result of years of experience watching the weather patterns in this area. I grew up near here, and when the sky is a certain color and the wind smells a certain way, I can tell that a storm is coming and when it will arrive. And Father Abbot has doubtless been at Nevarsin long enough to recognize at least some of the signs himself, so he didn't have to take my word entirely on faith."

Dyan smiled faintly. "And, besides," he said, "if you had *laran* you wouldn't have to be a Renunciate; you could have gone into a Tower instead."

"To give me equal protection from the men in my life, you mean?" Linnea inquired ironically.

"You shouldn't need protection from the men in your life," Dyan said primly. "They are supposed to protect you."

It would be cruel indeed, Linnea decided, to mention Dyan's father in this context, but she was developing a lively interest in how Dyan's mind worked. And since they would be spending several days on the trail together, it would help to know how far she could trust him. So she confined her response to a simple "why?"

"Because men are stronger than women."

"And you feel that it is the duty of the strong to protect the weak?"

"Of course it is," Dyan replied matter-of-factly. "Why have strength if you're not going to use it?"

"Some people seem to feel that strength should be used simply to get them what they want." Linnea remarked.

"No." Dyan shook his head definitely. "I'm not a *cristoforo*, but I have noticed that strength and burdens go together. And if you waste your strength on selfish gratification instead of doing the tasks your station in life lays upon you, then you become an object of pity at best, if not of contempt."

Presumably, Linnea thought, *he's thinking of his father, but he could just as well be describing mine. Well, at least he doesn't appear to share his father's tastes and weaknesses, and he isn't complaining about the trail or the pace we're setting. Still, I think it's about time to call a halt for the night.*

~oOo~

They made good time the next day and a half, and their journey was uneventful until they reached the bridge over the chasm that lay a half-league from Castle Ardais. But their luck ended there; the bridge was out, apparently collapsed under too much weight.

Linnea bit back a curse, not that she thought Dyan didn't know the phrase, but she had scruples about corrupting the young and supposedly innocent.

Dyan scowled at the chasm. "This wretched bridge falls about twice a year," he grumbled, "but did it have to be now?!"

He sat silently on his chervine for several long minutes, chewing on his lower lip and looking pale. Then he sighed. "*Mestra,*" he said slowly, "are you afraid of heights?"

Linnea, about to return a flip answer about the impossibility of living in the mountains and fearing heights, took a second look at his face. Heights didn't bother her much, but she strongly suspected that the same could not be said of her companion.

"I can handle them when I have to," she replied. "Why? Do you know another way across?"

"There's an old fallen tree trunk up that way a bit." Dyan gestured off to their right. "The tenants' children walk it on dares." From his tone of voice, it didn't appear to be a sport he participated in willingly.

"Well, we may as well go take a look at it," Linnea said. "There's no guarantee it's even still in place, but if it is, it could save us several hours—the next bridge over the chasm is at least two leagues downhill, isn't it?"

"Yes" Dyan said, turning his chervine and heading uphill. "And if we can get across the log, we come out right behind the castle. It's no particular military risk; it will barely hold an adult, and certainly not an armored man." He looked appraisingly at her. "It's a good thing you're small. We'll have to leave the chervines and packs on this side. If we get across, we can send the servants back for them."

~o0o~

They reached the log, and Linnea eyed it dubiously. It was about a foot in diameter and looked fairly sturdy, but its top was covered with snow, and there could easily be rot hidden under it. She considered roping Dyan and herself together and decided against it—too much chance of her dragging him down if the tree broke under her. She must outweigh him by a good thirty pounds.

"You'd best go first, Lord Dyan," she said. "You're lighter and have a better chance of making it—although I trust," she added, forcing a smile, "that if I fall, you will send a search party out after me."

Dyan's answering smile was even more forced than hers, and his skin had a distinctly greenish tinge to it.

"Remember," Linnea said bracingly, "we are not children playing 'I dare you.' Style and grace don't count; the object is to get across in one piece. I intend to straddle the trunk and crawl across—it may look silly, but I'm much less apt to get blown off or lose my balance that way."

Dyan considered that approach, and his color returned to normal. "We'll get wet, of course," he said, "but it's only a few minutes' walk to the castle and dry clothes." He tied the ends of his cloak around his waist, straddled the trunk, and shimmied across, dislodging a good deal of snow in the process.

"It seems solid enough," he called back from the other side. "Come ahead."

Linnea hiked her tunic a bit higher through her belt and started along the trunk. Halfway across, however, her tunic slipped and caught on something just behind her right hip, snagging her firmly into place. She twisted to try to free herself and almost overbalanced into the chasm.

"What's wrong?" Dyan called from the bank.

"My wretched tunic appears to be caught," Linnea said, trying to sound calm. "Why don't you go ahead to the castle and send somebody back to free me?"

"Somebody like a big, heavy adult?" Dyan asked skeptically. He took a deep breath and with a resolute expression on his face started crawling back across the log to her. In a moment he was practically in her lap. "Lock your ankles around the tree, brace yourself, and hold my waist," he ordered. "If you can hang onto me, I think I can reach back to where your tunic is snagged."

Linnea locked her legs tightly around the tree and clung to Dyan's wriggling body for dear life— both his and hers, if anything happened to him. After several uncomfortable moments, there was the sound of ripping cloth, and she was free. Dyan inched backward to a stable position and said carefully, "I think you can let go of me now."

Linnea cautiously loosened her grip, and Dyan pulled slowly free and wriggled backwards to the other side of the chasm. As soon as he was across, Linnea followed slowly, being very careful not to get her clothing snagged again.

Once on solid ground again, Linnea dusted the snow off herself and checked the damage to the tunic. Fortunately, it was just a rip in the hem.

"It's a good thing I wasn't wearing long skirts," she laughed nervously.

Dyan started to giggle. "And it's a good thing that I didn't have 'a proper escort'—can't you just see them trying to shimmy across that tree while holding their banners at the proper angle?"

Both of them burst out laughing at the picture that called to mind.

"Come along," Linnea said, as soon as she could speak again. "We'd better get indoors and into some dry clothes, and we need to send someone for the chervines."

"Follow me," Dyan said, "the path is this way." After a few steps he turned and looked back at her.

"Linnea? When I return to Nevarsin, will you escort me?"

"With pleasure, Lord Dyan," Linnea replied. "You're good company on the trail."

MEETING OF MINDS

Although this story was ultimately intended for the annual Darkover anthology, it was primarily written as a birthday gift for my youngest sister. Julie was keeping tropical fish at the time, and all the technical details came from her. And, no, I did not name my heroine after Disney's Little Mermaid—at least not consciously. This story also elicited my all-time favorite fan letter, which included the following: "I had terrible luck with my tropical fish. They all lived."

My Dear Father,

Cassilda's marriage to Edric Ridenow took place yesterday, so she is now Lady Serrais, which seems strange to me—she still looks like my big sister. It is really a shame that you and Mother could not be here for the wedding, but Coryn deputized for you admirably, and Donal and I were here to support and encourage Cassilda. She was really nervous before the ceremony, but she seems happy enough this morning.

Coryn and I will be remaining here until spring

because my *laran* has finally starting developing (I thought I'd never grow up, but it looks as though I will after all), and Auster, who came home from Arilinn for the wedding, says that I shouldn't try to travel while I'm still getting threshold sickness. Don't worry; I'm not sick enough for it to be dangerous; I just feel miserable.

I know that you and Mother have been concerned over what type of *laran* I'd develop, so I hasten to assure you that it won't be nearly as inconvenient as that of my brothers and sister. Even I remember how the hawks followed Cassilda around when her rapport with them developed. They made themselves terribly unpopular with Mother (to say nothing about how the servants felt about them) until Cassilda finally managed to break them of their quite natural impulse to perch on the edges of Mother's tapestry frame. And nobody is going to forget Donal's rapport with the wolves—especially how they all howled every time he got threshold sickness. At least Coryn's rapport with horses was comparatively quiet, and even useful, although you did have to add on to the stables that year.

I have developed rapport with animals, of course, but the animals in question are small, silent, and won't follow me around the house.

As you no doubt know, Lerrys Ridenow has traveled around the Empire, and he brought back a considerable number of small fish from the tropical seas of Terra. I have developed a rapport with the fish, and Lerrys has given me 500 of them for a Midwinter gift, which was really awfully nice of him. Donal will bring you with this letter the plans for the tanks which will be needed to house them. Most of the fish can go in the 200-gallon tank, but the tetraodons should have a tank to themselves, the anastomus are definitely too aggressive to be put in with any of the other fish, and the cichlids will kill off even each other, but I believe that if we put them by themselves in the 75-gallon tank I can persuade them to leave each other alone.

Coryn and I will bring the gravel, filters, and heaters when we come home, and Auster has very kindly volunteered to borrow the aircar from Arilinn to bring the fish home as soon as the weather gets warm enough (the fish die if the water they're in gets much colder than tropical temperatures on Terra—that's why all the tanks have to have heaters). The tanks should all fit along the wall in my bedroom that doesn't have windows or doors, but the heaters will probably have to go under the bed.

I hope that you and Mother had a good Midwinter, and I shall see you in the spring.

Your loving daughter,
Arielle MacAran

DESTINED FOR THE TOWER

by Elisabeth Waters & Deborah J. Ross

Deborah and I collaborated on this story, which was inspired by a line in *Sharra's Exile*. It was an interesting experience for her daughter. As we tossed plot ideas back and forth and argued about what would work best, Sarah looked at us as if we were crazy. I remember telling her that this was actually what plotting a story was like, but she normally didn't observe the process because it took place inside her mother's head.

Deborah published her own collection of Darkover stories, *A Heat Wave in the Hellers*, last year. As she didn't include this story in that book, we agreed that I would put it in here.

Diotima Ridenow wandered through a blue fog, searching for someone, someone important, she couldn't think who. There was something subtly, horribly wrong about the blue. Surely the overworld should be gray. She remembered she was looking for her mother, and her mother was dead. Did the dead feel so cold, as if they were encased in ice?

With every step now, it was harder to go on, as if her body were freezing solid. She could no longer move, could no longer feel her arms and legs. It became harder and harder to breathe. She wasn't breathing. Was she dead, too?

Before her lay a coffin. Expecting to see her mother, she peered into it. Inside, Ashara opened her ice-colored eyes and reached long thin arms toward her. Dio recoiled with a terrified scream....

She jerked awake and found herself sitting upright in her bed, shivering violently. Her blonde hair tumbled about her face. Around her, the Tower walls were hard and gray, still ringing with the echoes of her scream.

The door opened smoothly and her aunt Jerana glided in, a faded shadow of a woman in the crimson draperies of an Under-Keeper. Her brows creased slightly in disapproval.

"Dio, you know better than to leave your body without a monitor there to watch it. Surely by this stage of your training you know how dangerous that can be." She sat down on the foot of the bed, ignoring both the rumpled bedcovers and Dio's obvious distress.

Dio swallowed, trying to speak.

"We all know how disturbed you are by your mother's death," Jerana went on calmly. "It is particularly unfortunate that it should occur at this stage of your training. Later on you would have been able to deal with it better."

Dio looked into her aunt's eyes and noticed they were pale gray. Surely they'd been green when she was a girl. She shivered again, remembering the dream. "I saw... in the coffin... I saw Mother Ashara...."

"Of course you did. She's a mother to all of us. But I assure you, she is still very much with us. You need not worry, child; Mother Ashara will never leave you." Jerana tucked the covers around her niece with a firm hand. "Go to sleep now. You have a long journey ahead of you tomorrow, but you will be back among us and safe soon enough."

~o0o~

The next morning, Dio went to take her formal leave of Ashara, Keeper of Comyn Tower. Ashara's chamber was at the very top of the Tower, reached by some mysterious ancient machinery, a relic from the Ages of Chaos, which carried Dio up a smooth tunnel as if she were floating on a calm wind. As she entered Ashara's presence, Dio was struck by the immense, almost inhuman stillness that emanated from the room. It seemed unusually quiet today, almost as if she were the only living creature in this portion of the Tower.

Dio straightened her shoulders and composed her face into the proper neutrality for an Under-Keeper in training. This room always made her feel claustrophobic, which was odd because it appeared to be infinite. Daylight filtered through the translucent walls, making the figure of Ashara, sitting on her great carven glass throne and wearing a loose blue-grey robe, virtually invisible. Dio had the fanciful thought that the entire room was part of Ashara, that Ashara encompassed the room, rather than the other way around. She told herself uneasily that this notion was just a residue from her nightmare, and she stood quietly, waiting for Ashara to speak.

"My daughter." Ashara's voice flowed out across the room, seeming to come at Dio from all angles. As always, she felt surrounded, inundated by Ashara's presence.

"I am sorry for the death of your mother."

"Thank you," Dio murmured mechanically.

"It is particularly unfortunate that it should occur at this time. It is unusual for a Keeper to leave the tower at this point in her training, but I have no choice. Since you are not yet formally sworn to me, your duty to your family takes precedence."

"Yes, Mother Ashara," Dio said numbly.

"But it need not be too long a delay. You will return directly after Midsummer, and then you will take your Keeper's Oath."

Ashara's words, her very presence, clung to Dio as she was carried downward in the strange vertical shaft. She found herself remembering her aunt Jerana's words, "Mother Ashara will never leave you," but they filled her with uneasiness instead of comfort.

Nonsense, she told herself, *I'm just upset, that's all. Going home to Serrais for the funeral is a duty like any other, easily borne and soon passed. Then I'll be back and take my place as Ashara's Under-Keeper, as is my right as a* comynara. *It's what I've worked so hard all these years for....*

~oOo~

The day was bright and windy, and the roads muddy from last night's rain. Only a few miles out of Thendara, one of the guards spotted a party on the road ahead. Dio saw a flash of red-gold hair in the center of the group. Instantly she recognized Lerrys, her favorite of her five older brothers. He too would have been summoned to Serrais for the funeral, probably from a round of partying in Thendara.

She sent out a mental call. Lerrys spun his horse around and gave the order to halt. In a few minutes her party had drawn even with his.

"Little sister, how you've grown!" As usual, Lerrys was elegantly dressed, even in his most somber clothing. A smile crossed his fair, angular features. "You left for the Tower a child, and return to us a woman!"

"I am hardly returning to you," Dio replied with spirit. "Only a few days' visit to see our mother decently buried."

"And for Midsummer Festival, as much as Father will allow us," Lerrys said. He'd never lied to Dio as a child, and now he made no pretense of disguising his disappointment at missing the Festival in Thendara with his friends to pretend mourning for a woman he'd scarcely known. Lady Serrais had taken little interest in him as a child and none at all from the time she realized he had no intention of giving her grandsons. And she had been ill even before Dio had left for the Tower several years earlier, so her death now had come as no particular surprise.

Dio shook her head, her travel veils rippling in the wind. "You may be able to dance away most of the night and end it in any bed you wish, but Father will doubtless pack me off to my room after the first few dances. I'll be going back to the Tower the next morning to take my final Oath."

Lerrys gave her a quick, discerning glance, and she felt his mind brush briefly against hers. For a moment he was silent, thoughtful. "Are you sure that's what you really want, little sister?"

She opened her mouth to answer, but he'd already spurred his horse forward, mud splashing behind him. Dio, an enthusiastic rider, booted her horse into a gallop after him. Her chaperone, a young Tower technician, followed with a patient sigh.

~o0o~

They pushed on as far as possible that day, until the last rays of the red sun vanished behind the hills and they were forced to make camp. Dio climbed stiffly out of her saddle and handed the reins to one of the guards. She shocked her sedate, proper chaperone by helping to set up the tents and picket lines. After dinner, she sat with Lerrys around the dying fire, her face shadowed by Kyrrdis's blue light. She stretched and groaned.

"Sore muscles?" he asked, raising one eyebrow.

"Yes, but they're worth it. I'd forgotten how much I love riding."

"You always were a tomboy."

"A what?"

He grinned wickedly. "It's a *Terranan* term. Invented to describe you."

Dio made a face at him, feeling oddly childlike and free. It was good to be able to laugh and joke, to be with someone who was not trying to mold her into the image of a perfect Comyn Keeper. "At least we can be sure of one thing," she pointed out. "After today's ride, we'll all sleep well tonight."

~oOo~

In her dreams, Dio was once again a small child, watching the Festival Ball dancers with a mixture of delight and anticipation. This was the first year she had been allowed to attend at all, and she was so excited she could hardly stand still. Aunt Jerana danced past, her hair shining to match to gold trim of her elegant gown. Her eyes sparkled the same brilliant green as the full skirt that billowed about her as she spun in the intricate figures of the pattern dance. Dio watched, rapt in admiration; surely her aunt was the most beautiful lady in the room.

As the music came to an end, Jerana saw Dio watching from the corner and danced lightly over to her. "Are you enjoying this, little one?" she asked in a light, musical voice.

"Oh, yes," Dio replied enthusiastically. "It's wonderful! I wish I could dance like you."

Jerana laughed and scooped Dio up into her arms as the music started again. "So you shall, *chiya*." She whirled back into the pattern, still holding the child, and Dio laughed in delight.

But suddenly the room turned cold; she was so

cold. Blue fog swirled around them, shrouding the other dancers and muffling the sound of the music, which gradually faded into silence. The blue light grew stronger, and Jerana's eyes no longer brimmed with vivacious laughter and joy of being alive. Her face had gone inhumanly serene, without even the memory of a smile, and the color faded from her cheeks and eyes.

Now the blue fog was turning solid, like ice freezing from the outside in. Jerana danced on, unheeding, still holding Dio, but seemingly no longer aware of her. Dio looked around in wild desperation, searching for a way out. The blueness was faceted at the edges, smooth regular planes closing in on them. Horrified, Dio realized that they were in the center of a matrix.

She tried to call out for help, but her voice bounced back from the sides of the matrix, nearly deafening her with reverberations. Her words were trapped within the crystal, trapped as securely as her body in her aunt's arms.

She awoke, gasping, her face covered with cold sweat. Kyrrdis, now near descent, bathed her pallet in blue-green light through an opening in the tent. Her blankets lay heaped to one side. She must have tossed them off in her sleep. That was why she felt so cold, she told herself, the reason for her nightmare. Yet it was a long time before she could sleep again.

~oOo~

Throughout the next day's journey, the arrival at Serrais, and her mother's funeral, Lerrys's words echoed through Dio's mind. "Are you sure that's what you really want, little sister?"

Am I sure... She had never asked herself this question before. No one had ever asked it. It had been planned from the time she was born that she would go to the Tower to serve Mother Ashara and the Comyn, even as her aunt Jerana had done. She thought of her aunt, who had been gay and laughing when she played with her as a small child. When Dio first came to Comyn Tower, she had been surprised to find her aunt a stranger, pale and quiet in her red draperies, a faint shadow of her former self.

No, Dio realized with a shock. *Not of her former self. A faint shadow of Ashara. Is that what will happen to me?*

Suddenly she wanted very much not to return to the Tower in two days' time. Squaring her shoulders, she went in search of her father, who had retired to his study after the funeral and had been there all afternoon. She'd have just enough to time to speak to him before dinner.

The heat from the roaring fire struck her full in the face. Her father slumped in a chair nearby, an empty brandy glass in his hand. She went to him but did not reach out, the Keeper's habit of isolation already ingrained in her. He looked up, his eyes red-rimmed, whether with weeping or brandy she could not tell. If he had been anyone else, she would have sensed what he was feeling, but her father had always kept himself tightly barriered against his children. In fact, all members of her family had strong shields against their empathic gifts, although Lerrys sometimes allowed his to drop around her so they could talk mind to mind.

There was no graceful way to begin. "Father," she blurted out, "I don't want to go straight back to the Tower. I want to stay home for a while."

He blinked at her in surprise. "What? Whatever for?" He indicated a letter lying on his small secretary desk. "My sister writes that you are doing well, a credit to our family. She says you'll be taking your Oath as soon as you return."

Dio hesitated. "I'm not sure I'm ready for that."

"Surely Ashara and Jerana are better judges of that than you are," he said gruffly.

"But it's my life," Dio said slowly, "and I'm not sure I want to end up like Aunt Jerana. I remember what she was like before she went to the Tower—and you must remember even better than I. You saw her again when you took me there. She's not the same person, you must know that."

"Of course not," he replied impatiently. "She's a Keeper."

"But she's not Jerana anymore! Even her eyes are a different color!"

He scowled. "What are you talking about?"

"They used to be green, and now they're pale, blue-gray, like ice."

"Don't be silly, child." He got up and poured himself another glass of brandy from the decanter on the sideboard, turning his back on her. "Everyone's eyes fade as they get older."

Dio walked around him and locked her eyes with his. "Your eyes are still green, and you're older than she is."

"What difference does it make what color her eyes are? A Keeper's work is more important than her physical appearance. Jerana is a credit to her family and her caste, as you will be as soon as you get over this foolishness. It is a great honor to be chosen by Ashara. Do you know how few girls she finds suitable?"

"And have you ever wondered why that is?" Dio shot back. "And why so many of them fail the training? The other Towers don't even require a Keeper to remain a virgin all her life, and Ashara's training only starts there!"

Her father scowled fiercely at her. "Mind your tongue, girl. That is not a proper subject for discussion between father and daughter." Dio flushed and lowered her eyes. "Ashara trains Keepers in the old ways," he continued, "the ways that have kept the Towers strong for centuries. My sister was trained in that way, and my aunt before her; the daughters of our family have been Keepers, good Keepers, for generations. I'll not have you whining and asking impertinent questions about things that are none of your affair!"

Dio felt the blood burn within her veins. She lifted her chin and looked straight into her father's eyes. "You are saying that my life and my body are not my business. You know what happened to Aunt Jerana—whether you admit it or not—and what will happen to me, and you don't care!"

"Don't you dare talk to me like that!" her father thundered. "Go to your room and stay there until you remember your manners! And you are going back to the Tower, first thing in the morning after the Festival. I'd send you back this instant if I could!"

But then my escort would miss their Festival celebration in the village, Dio thought angrily, *and you care more for them than for me!* She whirled and ran from the room, slamming the door behind her.

~o0o~

Dio's anger spilled over into her dreams, for when

she found herself once more trapped in the blue matrix, she punched through the nearest faceted wall with her bare fist. It shattered with a satisfying crack, followed by a tinkling sound as the fragments tumbled to the floor. Heedless of her bare feet, she pushed her way through the opening, only to discover that there was no floor on the other side. She floated slowly downward, the shattered crystal receding above her head. Only then did she realize she was still in her nightgown, surrounded by the nearly featureless gray of the overworld.

In the distance she could see Comyn Tower, a steady blue light surrounded by the small firefly lights of the Thendaran matrix mechanics, but not all the imps in Zandru's forge could induce her to return there. She could see the flicker of other towers—Arilinn, Dalereuth, Neskaya, Corandolis—but she knew there was no help for her from any of them. Yet she could not remain here, in the overworld, for any length of time without discovery.

The next moment she found herself standing beside her mother's grave in the family burial ground at Serrais. "I wish you were still here, Mother," she whispered. "Father would listen to you." Cold tears began to trickle down her cheeks. "But then, you might simply tell me to obey my father."

She sighed, her anger draining away and leaving an almost paralyzing weariness in its wake. "Maybe I should obey him. It's what I've worked towards; it's all I know. And I would be a Keeper of Comyn Tower; they might even let me have Arilinn or Neskaya. Maybe it wouldn't be so bad—and it's not as if I have anywhere else to go." She stared down at the unresponsive mound of earth at her feet for several minutes before returning to the house. She walked through the door of her bedroom, where her body waited on the bed, but suddenly stopped, confronted by the mirror which stood directly opposite the door.

The reflection in the mirror was Ashara's. Dio gasped in horror, her hand flying to her mouth, and for an instant the reflection flickered and she saw herself, green eyes wide and staring and blonde hair hanging lank and loose about her shoulders. But as she watched, her expression grew calm, her hair changed to silver, her eyes faded from green through grey to ice-blue, and once again the image was Ashara's.

Dio woke once again sitting bolt upright in bed with her heart hammering. It took her several long minutes to get up the nerve to leave her bed and look in the mirror. The image in the mirror was her own, with no hint of Ashara visible. Still, Dio spent the remainder of the night pacing the floor and checking the mirror at frequent intervals.

~o0o~

With trembling hands, Dio pulled off the dress of soft blue wool embroidered with flaxen lilies which had been her only formal gown when she still lived at Serrais. The years in Thendara had added inches as well as curves to her body and there was no way she could appear in public wearing it. And if she had to remain in her room tonight, she would have no chance to speak to Lerrys, the one person who might conceivably help her, and she would be shipped back to Thendara in the morning just as surely as if she were a sheep for the slaughter. Close to tears, she rumpled the dress and threw it down in a heap.

Dio wrapped herself in an oversized dressing gown and stormed down the hallway. Perhaps some visiting lady had left a gown, out of style no doubt, but still wearable. In one of the guest bedrooms, she spied a huge old chest. She lifted the lid and reached in, pushing aside the heavy layers of cedar-scented fabric. She laid aside a heavy cloak in black wool trimmed with tatty fur, more suitable for a grandmother than... whatever she was. The dress beneath it was faded and carefully patched but clean. Evanda alone knew how it got there; it was the sort of cast-off a village girl might wear to Festival.

At the bottom of the chest, Dio spied

something in bright green and gold, the Ridenow colors. Hardly daring to breathe, she drew out the gown and held it up. The folds of rich fabric gleamed in the candlelight. The bodice tapered to a point, the skirt flared out, full and graceful. It was a dress fit for a *comynara*, and, yes, she thought it might fit.

Dio scooped up the gown, folded the village girl's dress in it, and hurried back to her room. She hid the dress under her travel cloak and rang for a maid to help lace her into the gown. When that was done and the maid off on another errand, she studied herself in the mirror. The gown fit perfectly, as if it had been made for her. She smiled at her image, and then frowned. There was something oddly familiar about the gown, but she had never worn one like it before. She pirouetted, watching the skirt billow around her, and suddenly it came to her where she had seen this dress before.

Jerana had worn it that Festival Night so long ago, Dio's first and Jerana's last. Jerana had worn it in her dream.

Dio's chin lifted in a gesture of defiance. She hoped her father would remember the dress, too. Tonight might be the last time he would permit her to wear the Ridenow green and gold. If so, she would wear them proudly.

~oOo~

The great hall at Serrais was full but slightly subdued in deference to the recent death. Some of the guests wore somber colors, but many had donned their usual Midsummer finery. After all, Lady Serrais had been decently buried, with all due solemnity and honor, and the Festival Ball came only once a year. Down in the village, the tenants and craftsmen held their own much less formal celebrations. There would be a new crop of village babies in seven months.

"I give it about two hours," Lerrys murmured to Dio as the pattern of the first dance carried them briefly together. "After that, Father will go to bed and everyone else will liven up."

Dio tossed her head and smiled absently at her partner, a portly, middle-aged man of impeccable propriety, a distant cousin. She waited until she was again close enough to Lerrys to whisper. "The first couples dance—with me!"

Lerrys raised one eyebrow speculatively but did not have an opportunity to reply.

Shortly afterwards, Lord Serrais retired to his ornately carved chair on the dais, signaling the end of the first round of formal set dances. The orchestra began a sedate tune, suitable for the older couples to dance together while they still had the energy. Moving with elegant grace, Lerrys returned his last partner to her female relatives and crossed the floor to Dio. His mouth curled in a sardonic smile as he bowed to her.

"The honor, dear sister?" Dio took his proffered hand with a sweeping curtsy. His hand around her waist was light but comforting. She leaned closer so that they could talk without being overheard.

"What is it, *chiya*?"

"Lerrys, I need your help!" she blurted out. "Father's going to send me back to the Tower and I'll never get away again. Ashara will take me over, just the way she did Aunt Jerana."

"Ahhh..." He glanced across the room, turbulent now with swirling plaids and skirts. "I was right, then." Dio could hear the pain behind his bantering words. Her brother's only value to Lord Serrais was as a father of sons, just as hers was as a Keeper.

Lerrys... She cried out with her mind. He flinched as if she had struck him.

"I'll stick by you, little sister. Do you want to run away, or are you going to just dig in your heels and refuse to go?"

She shrugged. "I don't have much choice. If I don't go to the Tower, Father won't want me here, either, will he?"

"We can always run away to Vainwal together and become professional dancers," Lerrys said lightly. "Unless you're desperate enough to become a Free Amazon."

Dio shuddered and grimaced. "I hope it won't come to that."

"It will be hard to hide you from Ashara."

"Unless Ashara doesn't want me anymore. But after that, nobody else might, either."

Lerrys looked sharply at her. "Whatever happens, you'll always be my sister."

The dance ended. As their hands parted, Dio sent Lerrys a mental message of gratitude. Lord Serrais had risen at the end of the dance and now he approached them. "Come, Diotima, it is time for us both to retire."

"Yes, Father," she murmured, dropping her eyes. She went quietly to her room, the perfect picture of a modest Comyn Keeper-in-Training.

~oOo~

Dio sat on the stone windowsill of her room, wearing the village girl's Festival dress. The night was unseasonably warm, even for Midsummer, and she'd opened the shutters. The great house lay about her, dark and still, but music and laughter from the village below floated up to her.

Above her, pearly Mormallor had risen to join its three companions. Dio recalled the old proverb, "Nobody remembers next day what was done under the four moons." In her case, she thought somberly, nobody would ever forget it.

She thought of the life she could never return to. Her father would be furious. He might even disown her. But then again, he might not, as long as she didn't get with child from this night, and she had training enough to prevent that. But Ashara would never take her back as a Keeper.

She was throwing away all the dreams she'd had, all the plans she had ever made, all the long years of work in the Tower. She might have been Lady of Thendara. Now she would be... what?

Dio. Dio and nobody else. She would have no more nightmares. She smiled faintly and picked up her shawl. Quietly she slipped out of the house and down to the village.

A CAPELLA

After living with MZB as she struggled her way though writing *Heirs of Hammerfell* (between multiple strokes), I really got to know the characters. When it came time to write that year's story, they were still with me, so I took a few of them and wrote a spin-off. Obviously, I was doing this with her permission; I wouldn't have dreamed of using them without it.

Domna Floria, newly returned to court to spend a time among Queen Antonella's ladies-in-waiting, walked slowly down the hall to the music room. Although the child she carried was not due for several months yet, she no longer felt inclined to skip down the polished marble corridor as she had as a child. Her father, Edric Elhalyn, had been Keeper of Thendara Tower as long as she could remember, so she had grown up in Thendara and spent a good deal of time at court.

Floria had worked at Thendara Tower as well, in the Keeper Renata's circle, until her marriage to

Conn of Hammerfell and her subsequent pregnancy made her unable to do the work of a *leronis*. She planned to return when her children were old enough not to need her, for *leroni* were always needed for Tower work, but now she was enjoying the chance to spend time quietly with her husband—or rather she had been doing so until King Aidan had summoned her to court.

Queen Antonella was recovering from a stroke she had suffered the previous year, and the King doubtless thought that the presence of Floria, who had always been a favorite of the Queen's, would cheer her. Conn, busy on the estates the King had recently granted him, had parted with his wife reluctantly, but he too was fond of King Aidan and Queen Antonella and wished them well.

And it isn't as if I had no friends here, Floria told herself, trying to cheer up. She seemed to feel blue all too frequently these days. The midwife said this feeling was normal and would go away after the baby's birth. *My mother-in-law and my father are both still working in the Tower here, my brothers are in town frequently, and Gavin Delleray is right here at court.*

At the thought of Gavin, she smiled. Gavin was unique. As the son of Queen Antonella's only sister, he doubtless would have been a favorite at court even had he been unremarkable, but nobody ever failed to notice Gavin. He was a talented composer, with a beautiful bass voice, and he had a flair for fashionable dress. But it was his custom of coloring his hair purple which people generally observed first. He and Conn's twin brother Alastair had been good friends since childhood, and they were all related, so he had formed one of Floria's circle of childhood playmates.

The best thing about being at court now, Floria thought, *is that I'll be able to hear the cantata he's written to celebrate Queen Antonella's recovery.* Floria loved music and thought quite highly of Gavin's talent, which was why she was heading toward the music room, hoping to catch at least part of his rehearsal.

The sounds she heard as she approached the room, however, bore no resemblance to any style she had ever heard Gavin use—or, for that matter, to any music she had ever heard anyone write, play, or sing. It sounded rather as though someone had made a viol using catgut strings without bothering to detach—or even sedate—the cat.

"No, *damisela*." Gavin's voice sounded terribly weary, as if he had said the words at least fifty times that morning. "That's still not quite the effect we're trying for. Why don't we take a break?"

"But I'm sure I can get it." The voice was female, shrill and high-pitched, but it sounded slightly better speaking than it had attempting to sing.

At least I assume she was attempting to sing, Floria thought. *I hope she isn't playing a cat-viol.*

"I'm sure you can," Gavin sounded anything but sure, "but I'm ready for a rest now." Gavin wasn't a terribly strong telepath, but even so Floria could hear his thoughts now. *Badly overdue for a rest—maybe even a permanent one.*

Floria opened the door and stepped into the music room. "Gavin," she called lightly, "may I interrupt you for a bit?"

"Floria!" Gavin greeted her with the air of a man lost in a blizzard sighting a guide. "Come and meet Capella Ridenow." The woman standing next to him smiled familiarly at Floria, although Floria was quite sure that they had never met.

Floria crossed the room warily, pasting a social smile on her face.

"So you're Floria," the woman chirped in an oddly girlish voice, "I'm so glad to meet you. Uncle Aidan and Aunt Antonella have so been looking forward to your arrival. Oh, you're pregnant," she babbled on, patting Floria's stomach. Floria recoiled, and Gavin stepped between them to block any further physical contact.

"Capella," he warned, "Floria is a telepath."

"That's nice," Capella babbled on heedlessly. "When is the baby due? I was born at mid-winter. Is it a boy or a girl? I'd want a girl. Or is it twins, like your husband and his brother? I think that's such a romantic story, the twin dukes of Hammerfell, separated in infancy—"

"Capella," Gavin interrupted her, "why don't you go tell Queen Antonella that Floria has arrived."

"Of course," Capella gushed. "I'll be so happy to tell her; Aunt Antonella will be so happy that you're finally here." She dashed from the room, narrowly avoiding a collision with the door, and clattered off down the hall.

"Aunt Antonella?" Floria said to Gavin as he carefully placed a comfortable chair behind her and extended an arm in case she needed support. She rested her fingertips lightly on his forearm as she sank gratefully into the armchair. "And the Queen knows I'm here; I've just come from seeing her."

Gavin sighed. "I had no intention of implying that you had failed in your duty toward the Queen; I just wanted to get Capella out of here for a bit. She's driving me insane, Floria; I swear it!"

Even at first acquaintance, Floria didn't doubt him. "Is she some kin of yours?" Floria tried to remember the women in the royal family. "Your mother was the Queen's only sister and you are an only child. And the King has no brothers or sisters. What exactly is her relationship to them?"

"Zandru only knows," Gavin sighed. "Even

Capella isn't stupid enough to call them aunt and uncle to their faces. She only does it behind their backs—she's an atrocious name-dropper."

"Quite," Floria agreed. "Is she married to one of the Ridenow sons? There must be at least six of them."

"Eight," Gavin corrected, "and five daughters. She's one of the daughters."

"You mean she isn't married?" Floria was surprised. "She must be at least thirty. But I can see how it might be difficult to find anyone willing to marry her. The Ridenow *donas* is empathy—but she doesn't even have the common courtesy to refrain from touching a telepath uninvited! To say nothing of her calling 'romantic' the fact that my husband and his brother were separated in infancy when their father was killed and their home burned over their heads, leaving each of them thinking the other dead."

"Actually, I have a theory about her," Gavin explained. "The Ridenow bred for empathy so that they could communicate with non-human species. I think Capella is the token non-human for the rest of the family to practice on."

Floria choked with laughter. "I really shouldn't laugh at her, and we shouldn't be making fun of her; I'm sure she's more to be pitied. She's obviously totally head-blind."

"And tone-deaf." Gavin groaned. "But she has

a half-brother who is some sort of *nedestro* connection of the King's—the exact relationship changes each time she tells the story, and he got a place for her at court. And somebody told the King she sang soprano, so she was assigned the soprano solo in my cantata."

He winced and collapsed into a chair next to Floria's. "How much did you hear as you came down the hall?"

"Enough to know she's not a baritone," Floria replied.

"I wish I had known you were going to be free of your Tower duties," Gavin sighed. "I'd have demanded *you* for the part instead. He looked at her hopefully. "Would you be willing to learn it? Please? Just so I can hear what it *ought* to sound like?"

"Of course," Floria said quickly, "I'd love to learn it. What are friends for?" They smiled at each other, sharing for a moment the perfect understanding that sometimes occurred between two telepaths. Then Gavin leapt to his feet, his energy and enthusiasm miraculously restored, thrust the score of the cantata into her hands and took up his *rryl*.

"Let's take it from the beginning," he said eagerly. "You don't have to sing full out, or even stand up if you don't want to; just mark it and see how much of it you can sight-read."

He played a few bars of introduction to indicate the tempo and nodded at Floria to indicate where the soprano solo began. Floria, whose sight-reading ability was quite good—especially when the composer was sitting next to her thinking hard about what the music ought to sound like—sang softly through the first section. She knew that her breath control was nowhere near what it ought to be—breathing was another thing that was more difficult when one was carrying a child—but her voice was clear and on pitch and she was managing the tempo quite well for a first run-through.

The clatter of hooves as a party of horsemen rode into the courtyard outside the window masked the sound of Capella's footsteps in the hall, but Capella barely gave them a glance as she dashed to the window, threw it open, and hung out to stare avidly down at the courtyard. "Isn't he beautiful?" she asked rapturously.

Floria stared questioningly at Gavin, who rose and went to look out the window himself. "Are you referring to old Lord Alton?" he asked in surprise.

"No, silly," Capella giggled, "his horse—the white stallion—isn't he gorgeous? Someday I'm going to have a horse just like him."

Gavin was speechless, and Floria couldn't think of anything to say either. It wasn't the first time she had seen a female human go into raptures over a horse, but it was the first time she had seen the phenomenon in a grown woman. Usually this condition manifested itself in girls of eight or nine and was outgrown by their middle teens—or sooner if a girl actually had much contact with horses. It was difficult to romanticize something that tried to eat every passing plant while you were riding it, stepped on your foot, shed long stiff hairs on your riding habit, and either refused to move at all, tried to scrape you off on a low branch, or bolted with you. Floria was an indifferent horsewoman, to say the least.

But simple politeness demanded that she say something. "Are you fond of horses, *damisela*?"

"Oh, yes," Capella instantly replied. "I'm going to have to get Lord Alton to let me ride that one—he's such a beauty!" Then she saw the music score in Floria's lap. "What are you doing with that?" she asked suspiciously.

"Gavin was just letting me look at it," Floria replied calmly. "He's been one of my favorite composers since we were children."

Capella still looked suspicious, but all she said was, "Aunt Antonella wants to see you, right now." She reached for Floria, obviously intending to drag her to her feet, but Gavin blocked her and dragged her aside, while Floria hastily pulled herself out of the chair.

"Capella," Gavin said in an urgent undertone, "Floria is a strong telepath. It is considered rude to touch a telepath without her invitation; most telepaths find contact with strangers painful. And Floria is carrying a child, which makes her even more sensitive."

"I know that!" Capella said defensively.

"Very well," Gavin said. "I shall escort you ladies to the Queen; I haven't seen her yet today." He extended an arm to each of them. Capella clung leech-like to his right arm, while Floria lightly rested her fingertips on his left sleeve, and they proceeded down the hall to the Queen's rooms.

When they arrived, they found King Aidan there, along with Lord Alton, who was paying his respects to the Queen and congratulating her on her recovery.

"Oh, Lord Alton," Capella said, barely managing to avoid interrupting his compliments to the Queen, "you must let me ride that beautiful stallion of yours!"

Lord Alton stared at her. *Obviously,* Floria thought, *he has not previously made her acquaintance either. Did the Ridenows keep her locked up in the attic until now?*

King Aidan tried to salvage the proprieties. "Lord Alton, permit me to present Capella Ridenow."

This should have been the Lord's cue to claim that it was a pleasure to meet the *damisela*, but this seemed to be beyond him at the moment. Floria wondered how often Capella had this effect on people.

"My stallion is a very dangerous animal, *damisela*," he finally said with a fair assumption of courtesy. "I must request that no one but his groom go near him."

"Of course," King Aidan endorsed his words. "I have already given orders to my head groom to have him stabled at the far end of the long stable, away from the other animals. If you have any problems with his stabling or my servants, Lord Alton, feel free to come to me with them."

Lord Alton nodded. "I thank Your Grace," he said formally. He bowed over Queen Antonella's hand, King Aidan kissed her cheek, and the two men departed.

"But animals love me!" Capella protested as the door closed behind them. "I'm sure I can ride the stallion!"

"It would be most discourteous to do so without his owner's permission," Queen Antonella said slowly. Her speech was still a trifle slurred from the stroke. It was perfectly understandable to Floria, but she suspected that Capella might understand only what she wished to understand. Queen Antonella looked troubled, as if she shared

Floria's suspicions.

"Floria," the Queen continued, "since you and Capella are my two youngest ladies at present, you will share a bedchamber."

Oh, no! Floria thought. Aloud she said simply, "I fear, Your Grace, that I am far from an ideal companion at night. The child I carry tends to make my nights rather restless, and I should dislike depriving Capella of her rest."

"Oh, don't worry," Capella cut in, "you won't disturb me in the slightest—I'm a very deep sleeper."

The Queen smiled faintly. "That's settled then," she said. "You girls may leave; I wish to speak to Gavin now. I shall see you at dinner."

Perforce Floria curtsied over the Queen's hand and withdrew, following Capella down the hall to the bedchamber allotted to them. Fortunately it was a fairly large room, and the two beds were on opposite sides of it. The maids had already unpacked Floria's things and put her favorite quilt, which she had brought with her, on her bed. She sank gratefully onto it and lay back against the pillows, feeling more tired than she would have believed possible. Capella was chattering away about something, but Floria fell asleep before she could figure out what it was.

~oOo~

Life at court quickly settled into a pattern. Floria got up early, while Capella still slept, ate breakfast with the court's few early risers, then sat with the Queen in the mornings (which spared her both Capella's company and having to listen to Capella rehearse). Capella and Gavin would both appear at luncheon, and Capella would sit with the Queen in the afternoons. Floria would take a nap after luncheon, enjoying the luxury of having their room to herself, and then go to the music room with Gavin, who insisted on teaching her his cantata "as an antidote to having to listen to Capella massacre it all morning."

"It is a shame," Floria agreed, making another notation in the copy of the score Gavin had made for her. "This is definitely the best thing you've done yet, Gavin. I hope that Conn will be able to come to court for the premiere; he'll want to hear this."

Gavin sighed. "If only I weren't stuck with Capella for the soprano. She's killing it, Floria, I swear it!"

"Surely she has improved at least a little since I last heard her," Floria said hopefully.

"No." Gavin shook his head. "It's incredible, but her performance hasn't changed a bit. Her consistency is amazing—she's convinced that she can sing and that she's doing it well, and she just does it the same way, over and over and over..."

He paced restlessly about the room. "It's horrible of me, I know, but I wish she would try to ride Lord Alton's stallion and get herself killed!"

Floria shuddered. "Don't remind me. She *is* trying; I've had to drag her back to our room three times this week."

Gavin stared at her. "What?"

"She sneaks out of our room, dressed for riding, in the middle of the night," Floria said grimly. "That's why the Queen has us sharing a room, so I can keep an eye on her."

"Poor Floria! No wonder you look so tired. I hope you don't have to drag her back by force."

Floria shook her head. "When I catch her, she claims she must have been sleep-walking."

Gavin looked incredulous. "Does she really expect you to believe that?"

Floria shrugged. "I don't care. As long as she uses that story, she has no excuse not to go straight back to bed when she gets caught, so it has its uses."

"It's a stupid game," Gavin said flatly.

"True," Floria sighed. "Shall we try this section again?" She indicated her score. "I think I almost have that long phrase correct."

They worked steadily on the cantata for the next several hours. In fact, they lost track of time, so they were surprised when Capella entered the room. "What are you doing here, Floria?" she asked shrilly. "It's time to dress for dinner; we'll be late. What was that you were singing?" She looked at the score Floria held, and turned on Gavin. "Why are you letting Floria sing that instead of teaching it to me? *I'm* singing the soprano part."

It was unfortunate that Gavin lost his temper at that. Understandable, but unfortunate. "I have been trying to teach this to you for the past month!" he roared. "But you won't bother to listen to anything anyone says; you insist that what you're doing—*I* wouldn't call it singing—is good; and then you don't even *recognize* your part when you hear it sung correctly!"

"That's not my part," Capella protested. "You haven't taught that section to me yet!"

"Oh, I've *taught* it," Gavin snarled. "You just haven't learned it. You're hopeless, and I'm going to the King and tell him so. I absolutely refuse to let you ruin my work—and I don't care whose bastard you *might* be distantly related to!" He stormed out of the room.

Capella stared after him with her mouth hanging open. "What's wrong with him?"

Floria sighed. She thought that Gavin had made his point fairly clear, probably to everyone in earshot—except Capella. "Shall we go dress for dinner, Capella?"

Capella regarded her through narrowed eyes. "*You're* doing this to me," she accused. "I'll stop you. I swear I'll stop you."

~o0o~

Life went on much as before, although Gavin had Floria working even harder on the cantata. He didn't speak of it, but Floria knew he hoped to persuade the King to let her substitute for Capella. Floria continued to keep an eye on Capella, especially in light of her threats, but Floria believed the threats to be empty ones until the afternoon she finished the solo and was startled by applause from the doorway.

"Brava!" Conn said, smiling at her.

"Conn!" Floria, moving faster than she had in weeks, ran into his arms. "What a wonderful surprise! Why didn't you tell me you were coming, and how long can you stay?"

Conn just held her for a moment, and Floria basked in his embrace. It felt rather like warm sunshine, only better.

Gavin set aside his *rryl*. "Good to see you, Conn," he said, getting up. "I'll leave you two alone now; I'm sure you have a lot to catch up on."

"No," Conn said, "I believe that we *three* have a lot to catch up on. Sit down, Gavin." Gavin did, and Conn, still holding Floria, sat down in the armchair with her on his lap. "Tell me, who is Capella Ridenow?"

Gavin groaned. "Words fail me; you'll have to meet her yourself."

Floria sighed. "She's one of the Ridenow daughters, currently serving as one of Queen Antonella's ladies. She's head-blind and tone-deaf, and she's supposed to be singing the soprano solo in Gavin's new cantata."

"My sympathies, Gavin," Conn said. "Is that what Floria was singing just now?"

"Yes," Gavin said. "Floria has kindly agreed to learn it so that I can hear what it should sound like. You can't imagine what that woman does to it!"

"She would appear to be a very unhappy person," Conn said quietly.

Floria twisted to look up at his face. "Have you met her?"

Conn shook his head. "She wrote me a letter."

Floria understood, but Conn had to explain to Gavin. "I can sense things by handling physical objects. Frequently-worn jewelry works best, but I can pick up quite a bit from a letter, especially when the writer is suffering from strong emotions at the time of writing."

"What did she write to you about?" Floria asked.

"She claimed," Conn said in a voice a bit

unsteady with laughter, "that you and Gavin were carrying on a flagrant affair and making a scandal at court and that she thought I ought to know about it."

Floria choked. "How kind of her," she said weakly.

Gavin was not amused. "That wretched, conniving, interfering, unscrupulous—"

"Calm down, Gavin," Floria said calmly. "You know as well as I do that Conn would never believe her nonsense."

"Certainly I trust my wife and my friends over some girl I've never heard of before," Conn said. "But it did provide me with an excuse to come to court and see you—and hear your new cantata, Gavin."

"If you want to hear it the way it should sound," Gavin snapped, "somebody will have to kill that stupid brat! It's bad enough that she thinks she can sing, but to try to slander Floria like this—it's outside of enough!"

"Has she been trying to sell this story to anyone but me?" Conn inquired.

"I don't think so," Floria replied. "I'm sure the Queen would have said something to me if Capella were trying to make this common gossip." She twisted reluctantly out of her husband's hold. "And speaking of the Queen, Conn, we had better go tell her you're here."

"True," Conn said. "I'm being horribly remiss in my manners; I ought to have paid my respects to her first—but I wanted to see you."

Floria smiled. "I think the Queen—and the King—will understand."

"I'm sure they will," Gavin agreed as they went out into the hall together. "Love is not hard to understand for those who have experienced it."

~o0o~

They heard angry shouting as they approached the Queen's rooms. Gavin and Floria exchanged anxious glances.

"That's Lord Alton," Gavin said.

Floria nodded, "I hope Capella hasn't been bothering his horse again—but I'll bet she has."

"Is that idiot I saw in the stables as I arrived Capella?" Conn asked. "A woman in her mid-thirties with frizzy red hair?"

"Sounds like her," Gavin said. "What was she doing?"

"Heading toward the back part of the stables—the part that generally isn't used. She appeared to be going to an assignation with someone."

"Not someone," Floria sighed, "something. Lord Alton has a white stallion—"

"You don't mean—" Conn began carefully.

Floria laughed. "No, she just wants to ride the

beast. Lord Alton says it's dangerous and forbade her, but..." She shrugged. "Capella's not good at listening to anything she doesn't want to hear."

They entered the Queen's rooms to discover that Capella was hearing it again.

"I told you that animal was dangerous," Lord Alton was shouting, "and I told you to stay away from him! And then I walk into the stable and find you in his stall!"

"You didn't have to hit him!" Capella screamed at him. "You're a brute and a bully!"

"I wouldn't have *had* to hit him if you hadn't gotten in the way. Don't you realize he was about to take a chunk out of your arm?"

"He was not!" Capella protested. "He *likes* me."

"That makes one of him," Gavin muttered *sotto voce*. Unfortunately, Capella heard him.

"You're all beastly and I hate you!" she screamed. "I wish I were dead!"

"Try to ride my horse again and you will be," Lord Alton said grimly.

Capella looked around for sympathy. Finding none, she burst into noisy tears and ran from the room.

There was silence for several minutes as the room's occupants regained their tempers, and pulse rates and breathing returned to normal.

Lord Alton turned to Queen Antonella. "Your

Grace, I do apologize for this scene—"

The Queen smiled faintly and shook her head.

"Nonsense," King Aidan said briskly. "Quite understandable reaction. That girl badly wants conduct." Then he looked at the group still frozen in the doorway. "Conn! Good to see you, dear boy! Come to see how your wife goes on, have you?"

Conn bowed over the King's hand, then the Queen's. "I ask your pardon for coming uninvited, but," he smiled ruefully at Floria, "I missed my wife."

"Floria is a lucky woman to have a husband who loves her," Queen Antonella said softly. She looked at Floria. "I suppose you want your room changed so you can be with him?"

"Yes, please, Your Grace," Floria said thankfully.

"Tell the servants to move your things while we're all at dinner," the Queen ordered. "Capella's probably there crying right now; no need to disturb her."

Floria nodded. *I'm sure Capella didn't intend it that way, but she did me a real favor, sending that silly letter to Conn.*

"Such a shame she hasn't married," the Queen went on. She looked at Gavin. "I don't suppose you'd consider it?"

Gavin shook his head firmly. "Not for

anything in the world. She's tone-deaf."

The King chuckled. "That certainly wouldn't do in *your* wife, would it?" He frowned. "Still, she must have *some* good qualities."

"I'm sure she thinks she has," Lord Alton said. He was calmer now; his voice was down to a growl.

"Sounds like she thinks she can ride," Conn pointed out.

"She also thinks she can sing," Gavin sighed, "but believe me, she can't."

"If she were as good with horses as she thinks she is, I'd marry her myself," Lord Alton remarked. "Good trait to fix in the bloodline."

Floria bit hard on a quivering lip. "And if you gave her free run of the stables, you wouldn't see her in the house much."

Lord Alton laughed outright, and the remaining tension in the room eased.

~o0o~

Capella was quiet at dinner, but her look was obviously intended to convey the idea that she was plotting revenge. Floria, happy in the results of Capella's last attempt at revenge, didn't worry about it.

The next morning Capella was missing—and so was Lord Alton's white stallion. Floria and Conn were sitting with the Queen when Gavin came in with the news. He appeared to find it hilarious.

"No," he reassured Queen Antonella, "she's not hurt a bit. It seems she actually was correct when she said that animals like her. At least that stallion does. King Aidan tracked her with his starstone, and she was riding that beast with just a halter. She hadn't even bothered with a saddle! Lord Alton was quite impressed. He's gone after her, and he's going to take her home and get her father's consent to their marriage."

"What about her consent?" Floria asked. "Just yesterday she called him a brute and a bully."

"She'll consent," Gavin prophesied. "Her father will see to that. He has too many children to indulge her whims when she actually gets a good offer."

Conn patted Floria's hand. "Don't worry about her, my dear. I'm sure she'll enjoy the prestige of being Lady Alton."

"You're right about *that*," Gavin agreed.

"Yes, I think you are," Floria said. "Anyway, I think she likes horses better than people, and Lord Alton has more horses than anyone else in the Domains. She should be happy enough."

"And I'm ecstatic!" Gavin said enthusiastically. "Now that Capella's gone, Floria can sing the soprano part in my cantata. I think this works out well for everyone."

A SONG FOR CAPELLA

After MZB died in 1999, there were no Darkover anthologies for quite a while. Vera Nazarian, one of "MZB's authors," had started a small press, and she brought the Sword and Sorceress series back after DAW stopped publishing them, but she ran into financial trouble around 2012, so the MZB Literary Works Trust took over the anthologies, and as long as it was having me edit S&S, they decided to get Deborah J. Ross to edit Darkover anthologies. They figured there was a demand for them, and they were right. But as Deborah and I started on *Stars of Darkover*—I agreed to help her with the first one—we discovered a bit of a problem. Leslie Fish had written a story version of her well-known song "The Horsetamer's Daughter," but it was 38,000 words long, which is more than a third of the entire book. Deborah didn't want to give that much space to only one story, so I said "Well, *Stars* is scheduled for more than a year away, and I can assemble an anthology around Leslie's story pretty quickly." So while Deborah finished *Stars of Darkover*, I did *Music of Darkover*. Even with Leslie providing about half the content, however, we still needed more stories, and we needed them quickly, so I wrote a sequel to "A Capella." I put both stories in *Music*, because the second one doesn't make much sense if you have read the first one.

"...she rode his horse, now he's riding her..." Gavin Delleray scowled down at his *rryl*.

Not only were the words totally unacceptable for the occasion for which this piece had been commissioned, but he didn't even like the tune. "Is there such a thing as composer's block?" he wondered aloud.

"Gavin?" An incredulous female voice came from the doorway behind him.

Gavin whirled about so quickly that he almost fell off the chair.

"Floria!" He rose quickly to his feet and set a comfortable chair for her next to his.

Domna Floria, one of Queen Antonella's ladies-in-waiting, lowered her extremely pregnant body into the chair and shifted until she found what passed for a comfortable position. "Please tell me, Gavin, that this is *not* the song you're writing for the celebration of the marriage of Capella Ridenow and Lord Alton."

Gavin sighed. "I wish I could." If someone had to catch him perpetrating this disaster, at least Floria wasn't likely to make trouble. She and her husband Conn of Hammerfell were two of his best friends. And Floria was sufficiently acquainted with Capella Ridenow to understand at least some of his difficulties. "I *know* it's horrible; the tune is banal at best, and the lyrics—"

"—can't be sung in mixed company, let alone at a formal celebration at court. Have you got anything else?" she asked hopefully.

"Just an attempt at a chorus: *Neigh*." He sang the word on a descending scale. It sounded as despairing as he felt.

"It's a shame she fell in love at first sight with his horse," Floria sighed.

Both of them fell silent, remembering Capella's rapturous description of the animal. The three of them had been here in the music room together when she first saw the horse—and Lord Alton— although she had paid scant heed to the rider at the time.

"You could do so much more with a cat." Floria grinned at him impishly and sang *Me-ee-ow*, varying the pitches and dragging out the last syllable.

Inspiration struck. Gavin twisted to reach the paper and pen on the table beside him and started to scribble frantically, occasionally playing a bit on the *ryl* in his lap to be sure that what he was scribbling sounded correct when he played it. Floria sat quietly and did not interrupt him, although he could feel a low-level telepathic hum of encouragement from her.

He didn't know how long he worked, but when he came back to his normal self the sun had moved noticeably across the sky. Floria looked at him expectantly.

"Do you want to hear it?" he asked.

"Of course I do!"

"Remember, it's still rough," he warned. "But I think with some polishing it will be perfect for what I have in mind."

He sang it through in a light falsetto—the piece was written for two sopranos, and he knew just the two he wanted. "Are you acquainted with Javanne Ardais and Melitta Ardais-Hastur?"

"Oh, my paws and whiskers!" Floria laughed until she got the hiccups. "Calling *those* two 'cats' would be a fair description. What are you going to call the piece?"

"*A Duel for Two Cats*—what else?"

"And how are you going to get them to agree to sing it?"

"Oh, I'm not going to ask them to learn this." Gavin grinned evilly. "They'd not only refuse, they'd kill me. But, given the way they brag about their ability to perform anything at first sight..."

"You're *not* going to hand this to them during the celebration, in front of the entire court, are you?"

"Probably," Gavin admitted. "By the time I'm done with it, this will be a brilliant exhibition of technique, so even if they do figure out what the lyrics are, they'll forgive me. Probably."

Floria sighed. "They're vain, self-centered, and convinced that the world should bow down to them because they're so talented, but they're not totally stupid. It's going to be *when* they figure it out, not *if.* You had better have a good excuse ready. And in the meanwhile, have you got *anything* more on the song you're supposed to be writing?"

"Nay." Gavin shook his head.

Floria groaned at the pun. "You're in trouble, my friend. The celebration is next week. Lord and Lady Alton are due to arrive in two days, and you know Capella will want to hear what you've come up with."

"I'll tell her that I'm saving its debut for the celebration and couldn't possible play it for her before then."

"And she'll nag you unmercifully," Floria predicted. "Maybe her presence will inspire you."

Gavin groaned. "Is it too late for me to go on a visit to your brother-in-law in the Hellers?"

"Much too late. Besides, Alistair and his wife are coming here for the celebration. He *is* one of your oldest friends, and *she* isn't breeding." Floria looked down at her hand, which lay lovingly across her protruding belly. "It's not that I don't love our child, and Conn does too, but carrying the future is tiring and not conducive to travel."

"'Carrying the future'," Gavin repeated thoughtfully. "Didn't Lord Alton decide to marry Capella when he discovered that she could ride that stallion of his?"

"He said he'd marry her if she could really ride it when none of us believed her claim that she could," Floria remembered. "He said it would be a good trait to fix in the bloodline."

"A romantic to his fingertips," Gavin said ironically.

Floria knew who the true romantic in the room was. "Perhaps that's your problem, Gavin; the story isn't romantic enough for you. Could you get away with a comic ballad?"

"I don't know, but I'm desperate enough to consider anything. Have you got an idea?"

"Well," Floria sighed, "this is *really* weak, but... what if he's trying to ask her to marry him—"

"He asked her father, not her," Gavin objected.

"Haven't we already agreed that the real circumstances of the marriage aren't going to work here?"

"Sorry. Go on."

"So he's talking to her, but she's speaking in horse language. He asks her, and she says 'neigh' like a horse, but what he hears is 'nay' as in 'no'."

Gavin picked up the *ryl*, and started strumming something vaguely reminiscent of a drinking song. Then he started to sing.

"Marry me," Lord Alton said.
And Capella answered, "Neigh."

"I might be able to do something with it." He sighed. "I'll sleep on it tonight and see if anything comes to my dreaming mind. Gods know my waking mind isn't doing very much."

~o0o~

"No luck?" Floria asked the next day, surveying the balls of crumpled paper scattered on the floor all around him.

"None," Gavin replied, running an ink-stained hand through his already disordered hair. Given the fact that Gavin was the most admired dandy in Thendara and was well-known to be meticulous about his clothing and appearance, this spoke volumes about his state of mind. "And Capella will be here tomorrow, and you're right—she's sure to march straight in here and demand to hear 'her' song." He looked around wildly. "I need to find someplace to hide!"

"Don't try the stables," Floria said. "She may not go looking for you there—"

Gavin raised his brows. "*Nobody* would look for me in the stables."

"That's certainly true," Floria acknowledged. "But Capella spends so much time there that she'd probably find you even if she wasn't looking for you."

"So where should I hide?"

"Take what you need and lock yourself in your room," Floria suggested. Your valet can fetch meals for you for a few days, and even Capella won't dare go into the wing that holds nothing but bachelors' quarters. You can stay there until the celebration if you have to, just as long as you have something ready to perform when you come out."

"I think I'll have to do that," Gavin said. "I tried your idea last night, but—" He slumped in the chair, shaking his head. "Comedy might be a good solution to the problem, but I just can't regard the topic as comic!"

"You'd be fine if it were a love match," Floria said. "Look at the songs you wrote for me and Conn."

They sat in silence for several minutes, and then Floria added, "At least it's probably a reasonably happy marriage, even if they both prefer the horse to each other."

Gavin sat up straight. "That's it! I'll write about the horse! You carry the future for you and Conn, but when it comes to Capella and Lord Alton, it's definitely the horse that carries their future."

"You're right," Floria grinned at him. "It *is* a love match. They both love the horse!"

~o0o~

Gavin still locked himself in his rooms—with his *ryl* and a quantity of paper—and did not emerge until the evening of the celebration. When they gathered for dinner he appeared, once more the elegant dandy, with no sign of the strain of the previous week.

The concert went well. *A Duel for Two Cats* (listed under a different title in the program) was received with loud applause from courtiers too well-trained to laugh out loud in public. If either of the singers had figured out Gavin's joke yet, they were being careful not to show it.

Gavin's romantic ballad in honor of the marriage of Capella Ridenow to Lord Alton was the last number of the evening. It was a good thing that nobody had to follow that act, because the song was beautiful, and Gavin's performance was enthralling. It was a romantic portrayal of two people drawn together by shared interests—and a very special horse.

As Gavin's voice trailed off into silence, Capella sat clutching her husband's hand while tears streamed down her cheeks. Floria blinked back her own tears. Gavin had truly outdone himself.

The highest accolade, however, came from Lord Alton. "Good song, Delleray. Never knew you were so fond of horses."

THREADS

by Elisabeth Waters & Ann Sharp

Through years of Darkover anthologies, Ann Sharp had told me about a story she wanted to write for one of them. When Deborah and I were working on *Stars of Darkover*, I told Ann that now was the time. We agreed to collaborate on it, and I quickly learned that Ann can come up with great ideas and characters, but plotting is not something that comes easily to her. Between us, however, we can create a pretty good story—not to mention having fun with it.

"Sare, I have had an offer for you," her father said. Sare looked up with interest, until he continued, "—from Varlach." The expression on her face promptly turned to horror. Between them she and her mother had persuaded her father to turn down suitors from half the families in town—all of them more interested in Sare's dowry and the political and business connections with her father than in Sare herself. She was pretty enough, but not a beauty. But Varlach had money and connections of his own, although apparently not enough to suit him.

"I don't want to marry Varlach," she protested. "He has six wives already."

"Five," her mother corrected, looking up from the sewing in her lap. "Another one died in childbirth last week and the babe with her. His senior wife told me that he didn't particularly care—the babe was only a female." She frowned. "He really should stop marrying such small girls; the babies he fathers are too large for the type of girl he fancies to give birth to safely." She looked pointedly from her narrow-hipped daughter to her husband.

He sighed. "I'm not in favor of the match, but Sare has been putting off marriage for so long that it's getting difficult to refuse a reasonable offer. Varlach may have a dozen wives, but he can well afford to support them."

"Especially since seven of them are dead now," his wife said.

"That many?" He looked worried. "Sare, is there any man that you *would* be willing to marry? There are other offers, but he's the most difficult of them to refuse without offending."

"Well," Sare temporized, "it's hard to find a man who can equal my father. Do you realize that Mother and I are the only women in Daillon who

can stretch our arms wide enough to hug you?"
She reached out to the side with both arms,
demonstrating that she could extend them fully
without being stopped by the chain that ran from
wrist to wrist, passing through a loop on her belt.
"If I married Varlach, I'd be reduced to using one
arm—my other hand would be stuck at my waist."

"I can see the value of not offending him," her
mother agreed, "but I don't really want him as
part of our family."

"What about calling a Suitor's Challenge?" Sare
suggested. "If there are multiple offers, then there
will be other families to help enforce the
decision—at least until the final trial."

"And by then there will be precedent and a
loss of *kihar* to anyone who objects," her mother
added. "You could start with simple, crowd-
pleasing contests to narrow the field: footraces
and such. Once it's down to the last candidates,
then hold the Three Final Trials."

Her husband looked at her fondly. "I suspect
you can probably plan the entire event better than
I can."

"I'm certain my sewing circle will be happy to
assist me," she said demurely, but Sare saw the
smile they exchanged.

That's why I want Erald. That's *what I want in my
marriage.*

~oOo~

The traditional Three Final Trials tested skills useful to support a man and his family. The First Trial sent the contestants into the Dry Lands with instructions to return with provender, demonstrating the ability to survive themselves and to feed others.

Late that afternoon Sare and her mother sat behind her father as the contestants returned and he recorded the haul. Sare's part in this trial was to cook for the men in town from the ingredients provided.

A number of young men had made no provision to drink, guaranteeing a short and unpleasant survival time. An interesting collection of plant leaves, stems, roots, buds, and flowers told her the stillroom would be well stocked with the inedible choices. She spotted what looked like an entire colony of smoked insects and a plant whose nuts would cause double vision for at least the next two days. *Could I feed some of them to Varlach? I'm pretty sure he was the one who brought them. No, better not. Either he doesn't know what they are—or he does and is counting on my being ignorant enough to take out some of his competitors.*

There were also leaves which, if added to a common dish, would have the diners itching all the way from the mouth to the stomach. Varlach's pickings also included a sand-snake, an unidentifiable plant with oozing milky sap, and two endangered species of mushroom.

Erald had returned with a small critter, tubers, and—*where did he find it?*—spine-puff bloom stems, and a generous pail of juice from the spine-puff's barrel.

Sare cooked an ample meal from the ingredients provided, and everyone enjoyed Erald's desert rodent, broiled on skewers in alternate chunks of fresh meat, browned fat, slices of parboiled tuber and green hot-berry, accompanied by slices of baked spine-puff stems and hard-cooked sandbird egg slices, with spine-puff juice and desert tea to drink. Varlach seemed happy to eat what his rival had provided. *Of course, he doesn't know that Erald is the one I want to marry. He probably thinks I'm thrilled beyond words by his offer and that father is just using the Trials to get more influence in the city.*

Even the fact that Erald was chosen as winner of the First Trial by popular acclaim didn't seem to disturb Varlach. *He has something planned for tomorrow. I'm sure of it.*

~oOo~

The Second Trial, which Sare was not expected to watch, tested fighting skills. Sare had planned to watch through the lattice-work covering the windows on the upper floors. Her mother, inexplicably, had decided that Sare should be progressing on her sewing and made certain that she did, using the patch design of her half-finished coverlet to illustrate the progress of a contest where contestants were steadily eliminated. Only after her stint was completed and she had threaded all the sturdiest needles, normally used for leather, onto a hank of heavy thread, could Sare slip away to where she could overlook her father in a crowd of other men. At first it seemed just a confusing mass, but then she could tell that the men were in several groups. She saw Varlach, Erald, and several others, each apparently surrounded by friends or backers. She noticed with interest that one of Erald's backers was the brother of Varlach's late sixth wife. Sare didn't understand the rules, but she did observe that Varlach, wider and heavier than most of the others, probably should not have assumed that age and experience would necessarily prevail. Continuing on to treachery did not improve matters for him, and only confirmed what Sare had expected. *He did know what that plant was, and he expected fewer men to be able to fight today.*

Voices bellowed, "Foul!" loudly enough that she could hear them. Her father and two of her uncles joined Varlach's group, listened to excited talk, and then conferred. Then three of the men—

Erald, Varlach, and a third she couldn't recognize from her vantage point—were led to a side table and presented with drinks. Everyone else followed and conversation clearly became general.

When her father came in for supper, Sare asked about the results of the Second Trial. His lips tightened, and he said only, "I hope young Erald wins tomorrow."

"So does Sare," her mother remarked.

Her father raised his eyebrows. "I approve your taste, Daughter, but could you not have told me you favored him *earlier*? Last year, perhaps?"

~oOo~

The Third Trial demonstrated the ability of the suitor to provide shelter for his bride. It also demonstrated the antiquity of the Trials, for the requirement was tent-making. Each of the three remaining candidates was given several pieces of leather to be sewn into a tent. As the pieces—and the finished tent—were the same size, the Trial was judged on speed and workmanship. Sare sat on a leather cushion in the middle of the group, all of them surrounded by what seemed like the entire population of Daillon.

This is it. At least there are plenty of witnesses, so Varlach will have trouble cheating. She pulled the first needle from the hank of thread she had prepared yesterday, picked up the spool from which all of the thread used in this Trial would come, looked up at Varlach, fluttered her eyelashes, and asked "Would you like a long piece of thread, or a short one?"

As she had expected—and rather counted on—he asked for a piece of thread the length of her arm, adding that she would see soon enough something else that was long. Under cover of a lot of ribald comments from the men around him, she turned to the next contestant. He smiled and murmured quietly, "About half that length."

She gave it to him and turned to Erald, who leaned in so she could hear him through the jokes and said softly, "Minx! Give me the best length for this job. I'm not stupid enough to think the length of thread I use says anything about my virility. Besides, I've watched my mother sew. Just keep a new needle threaded and ready when I need it."

Sare handed him a needle with the shortest thread of the three and prepared a second one the same length, sticking it into her cushion where he could reach it easily. As she prepared additional threads for the other two men, she looked around her. The men were still joking about items of various lengths, but every woman in the crowd was either watching the contestants—some with looks of horrified fascination—or staring firmly at the ground with a carefully expressionless face.

Erald was on his fifth thread, quickly stitching

neat seams along the leather, and Sare was about to hand a second thread to the man she was now fairly certain had never been one of *her* suitors. She was looking around the crowd again—*anywhere but at Varlach!*—when she noticed a girl watching the third man while speaking into the ear of a man who was obviously her father. She handed over the thread and said softly, "It's not *my* father you're trying to impress, is it?"

He shook his head. "No, it's not. But I'm not the one you want to impress him."

"No. I'll make your next thread a little shorter if you like; it's easier to sew with a shorter thread."

"Thank you." He cast a glance at Erald's quick movements and bent over his work again.

He's doing nice work, and he listens. I hope she gets him—or he gets her.

Varlach growled, and Sare looked over to see if he was ready for another long piece of thread. Her eyes widened, and she hastily lowered her gaze to her lap. Not only had his thread knotted, as she— and every other woman in town—could have told him would happen, but he had caught the end of his sleeve in one of the knots.

Someone in the crowd, perhaps one of the brothers of Varlach's late wife, remarked that some long tools were obviously not as useful as their wielders believed. That was greeted with chuckles from the men that turned to full-blown laughter as Varlach stubbornly carried on a losing battle with his thread.

"Don't *you* laugh," Sare's mother whispered grimly as she came to give her another spool of thread. "You still have to live in the same town with him."

"Yes, Mother. I'll leave him with what *kihar* remains to him."

~o0o~

Sare didn't laugh. Erald finished his tent, and it was inspected. After he was proclaimed the winner and her father placed her hand in his, she did permit herself a smile.

It wasn't until she and her parents were safely indoors, having supper with Erald, that she finally broke. "I asked him how long he wanted the thread to be," she protested, "and I gave him exactly what he asked for!"

The whole table broke into gales of laughter. "You certainly did," her father said, "and plenty of people heard your question and his answer. I believe that Varlach will be taking a trading caravan out very soon."

"So his senior wife tells me," Sare's mother said. "He was going to wait, but now that he's not getting married right away..."

"I wish him a long and prosperous journey," Sare said sincerely.

SKI THE HELLERS

Back when I first started working for MZB, the Friends of Darkover had "Ski the Hellers" bumper stickers. I didn't have a car, but the bumper sticker made it very easy to spot my suitcase on an airport luggage carousel.

Tired of the same crowded excursions? For those looking for a completely new challenge, try a truly out-of-this world voyage! Journey to a new, unspoiled world, far off the beaten track, and ski its pristine mountains! This unique trip will be the adventure of a lifetime!

Review: 0 stars
My father gave this trip to my death-defying-sports-mad brother for his birthday. I was sent along with him because I believe there should be a difference between "extreme sports" and suicide. My brother thinks he's immortal.

I was uneasy even before we left, because I

had never heard of the agency arranging this trip, and I thought I knew the name of every company that arranged crazy excursions after years of listening to my brother and his friends plan their trips. It turns out I was right to worry.

The "new, unspoiled world" is a Class 4 Closed World, where it snows year-round and even the locals aren't crazy enough to ski for fun. The mountains are called the Hellers (and the name *does* come from the old Terran world for the place where bad people go when they die). The temperatures they told us to dress for were nowhere near as cold as the actual temperatures (the native religion has nine hells, each colder than the one before it), so we were starting to get hypothermia as soon as the shuttle dropped us off—just the two of us, with no guide, at the top of a mountain shortly before dawn. The way the shuttle took off, I'm pretty sure they were trying to get it out of sight before anyone saw it.

The pilot warned us that the locals were primitive and might be hostile, but I suspect that this really meant "we don't want them—or you—to find out how many laws we're breaking." (I didn't have to wonder how many safety rules they were breaking.) My brother was given a "panic button" to use if necessary, and he was not the one of us likely to use it. The plan was for us to ski down the "pristine" (no skiing trails) mountain and meet the shuttle after sunset. I had the hand-drawn map that was supposed to show us the meeting place, but I'm not sure I could have found it even if all had gone as planned.

My brother went zipping off downslope, and I followed more cautiously, thinking that, since nobody knew where we were, a fall could easily be fatal. I was right. I found my brother partway down the mountain with a compound fracture of his left leg and a concussion from hitting his head. He had been going so fast that even his helmet hadn't kept his brain from getting scrambled. The panic button was either non-functional to begin with or had been damaged when he fell. I couldn't move him, and I had no way to call for help, so I was pretty frantic. Also, as soon as I stopped moving my body temperature dropped to dangerous levels.

What saved us were the "primitive" and "hostile" natives, who turned out to be neither. While I don't think they were thrilled to find us trespassing, they did rescue us and turn us over to the Terran authorities at Thendara. This world is *not* "far off the beaten track." It's at a very strategic location, and the locals allow the Terrans to have one spaceport on the planet. Going anywhere other than the spaceport is Not Allowed. It's probably just as well that my brother had a broken leg, because healing and rehab kept him busy during the months it took to contact Father and have him pay our fines and arrange for us to be sent home.

I would report this agency to the licensing boards and business councils on every world where they advertise, but the Terran authorities here assure me they will take care of that.

ABOUT THE AUTHOR

Elisabeth Waters sold her first short story in 1980 to Marion Zimmer Bradley for *The Keeper's Price*, the first of the Darkover anthologies. She then went on to sell dozens of short stories to a variety of anthologies. Her first novel, a fantasy called *Changing Fate*, was awarded the 1989 Gryphon Award. *Mending Fate* is the sequel to it. Although she has stopped editing the *Sword and Sorceress* anthologies, Elisabeth still writes the occasional short story, usually for Mercedes Lackey's Valdemar anthologies.

She also worked as a supernumerary with the San Francisco Opera from 1983 to 1989, where she appeared in *La Gioconda* (twice), *Manon Lescaut*, *Madama Butterfly*, *Khovanschina*, *Das Rheingold* (twice), *Werther*, and *Idomeneo*.

She has stayed at home since March 2020, complying with San Francisco's various stay-at-home orders. Not only has she avoided catching Covid-19, she's also missed this year's flu strains and the common cold.

www.ingramcontent.com/pod-product-compliance
Lightning Source LLC
Chambersburg PA
CBHW070557180626
46817CB00005B/1883